THINK WOLF

THINK WOLF

Michael Gregorio

This first world edition published 2016
in Great Britain and the USA by
SEVERN HOUSE PUBLISHERS LTD of
19 Cedar Road, Sutton, Surrey, England, SM2 5DA.
Trade paperback edition first published
in Great Britain and the USA 2016 by
SEVERN HOUSE PUBLISHERS LTD

British Library Cataloguing in Publication Data
A CIP catalogue record for this title is available from the British Library.

ISBN-13: 978-0-7278-8611-8 (cased)
ISBN-13: 978-1-84751-706-7 (trade paper)
ISBN-13: 978-1-78010-767-7 (e-book)

All Severn House titles are printed on acid-free paper.

Severn House Publishers support the Forest Stewardship Council™ [FSC™],
the leading international forest certification organisation.
All our titles that are printed on FSC certified paper carry the FSC logo.

Typeset by Palimpsest Book Production Ltd.,
Falkirk, Stirlingshire, Scotland.
Printed and bound in Great Britain by
TJ International, Padstow, Cornwall.

For Roberta Barberini

ACKNOWLEDGEMENTS

We wish to thank Professor Bernardino Ragni of the University of Perugia for generously sharing his expert knowledge of wolves with us.

MAIN CHARACTERS

POLICE (in order of rank)
Lucia Grossi, Captain, Regional Crime Squad of Umbria
Jerry Esposito, Captain, Regional Crime Squad of Umbria
Antonio Sustrico, Brigadier, commander of *carabinieri* in Spoleto
Mario Pulenti, Special Constable, *carabiniere*
Michele Carosio, Special Constable, *carabiniere*

NATIONAL PARK POLICE
Alberto Bruni, Park Director
Mario Simonetti, Executive Park Ranger
Marzio Diamante, Senior Ranger (western sector)
Sebastiano Cangio, Park Ranger (western sector)

CRIMINALS
Don Michele Cucciarilli, 'Ndrangheta clan boss, Calabria
Simone Candelora, 'Ndrangheta lieutenant in Umbria
Ettore Pallucchi, 'Ndrangheta soldier in Umbria

CHINATOWN
Li Liü Gong, Chinese businessman, London
Heng Lu, Chinese restaurant owner, Foligno

CIVILIANS
Loredana Salvini, Seb Cangio's girlfriend
Manlio and Teo Pastore, truffle hunters
Linda Diamante, wife of Marzio Diamante
Maria Gatti, medium and fortune teller
Arnaldo Capaldi, bank employee

LA MATTANZA

The *mattanza* is still practised in the south of Italy.
The word derives from the vulgar Latin *mattar*,
which means *to kill*.
Shoals of tuna are lured inside an encircling net
which is known as the 'death chamber'.
When the trap is closed there is no escape.
Fishermen move in with clubs and the slaughter begins.

TWO YEARS BEFORE

Umbria, Italy.

A cold breeze sweeps down from the summit of Mount Bacugno.

Three shadows pick their way through the forest on the lower slopes. Whenever the moon slips behind the clouds, the silver footpath fades before their eyes, yet still they struggle on like blind men in a bad dream, their movements hampered after a hard night's work.

Somewhere, a lark trills, announcing the dawn.

Then distant thunder sounds, and the earth begins to shake.

They know the moods of the forest by night, the groaning trees, the rustling leaves, the cries of nightbirds. But these are not the sounds of the trees, the wind or the river down in the valley below.

The shadows freeze, draw close, trying to gauge the danger, trying to pinpoint where the noise is coming from, growing louder each moment like an earthquake rumbling beneath their feet. Then something rockets out of the undergrowth, grunting and roaring, hurtling straight at them, driving between them.

The one in the middle takes the blow, the others knocked aside like skittles.

It is over in an instant, the danger gone.

The sound of charging hooves soon fades. The rasping of the figure on the ground grows hoarse and frantic as silence reclaims the forest. A plastic lighter flares. The gash is longer than a handspan, the left thigh ripped and torn, blood spurting out of a severed artery, spraying their hands and faces, painting them black in the darkness.

They step back as a shriek rends the air.

Their eyes meet.

No word is said. A tool is raised – a long wooden shaft, an adze-like blade with two curved fangs at the back, like a *carpenter's hammer – and a mighty blow strikes the skull. They wait for a minute, watching for any sign of life, then they go to work with machetes, hacking at the arms and legs, the torso and head, chopping the sections into smaller pieces.*

As the first rays of sun crest the peak of Mount Bacugno, they dig holes in the damp, loamy earth and do what needs to be done.

ONE

Calabria, southern Italy.

Simone Candelora lay flat on a ridge, elbows propped on cold stone.

Lago Cecità stretched away from right to left, east to west, a pale moon glinting off the vast expanse of water. He couldn't see the mountains on the far side of the lake. It was pitch black over that way, just one or two lights that might have been stars but were really farmhouses scattered over the mountainside. It was a strange name for a lake.

Lake Blindness . . .

Who the hell had thought that one up?

He twisted the ring of the binoculars, focused on the farmhouse below.

Everything looked peaceful down there, but the knot in his stomach told him differently. The *carabinieri* manning the road-block out near Taverna had looked peaceful, too, telling him the road was closed, and that there had been a 'serious accident'. Their bulletproof vests and submachine guns had told him another story. Something was going on, and he had the feeling he wasn't going to like it.

He had volunteered for the job that night, wanting to shine in Don Michele's eyes.

He checked his watch, a cheap-looking Nite Speed chronograph, but accurate. He never wore the Rolex when he was working. Don Michele had warned him in that rough accent of his: 'Keep that Rollie out of sight, Simò. The cops are fond of those.'

The others had laughed at the joke, the suggestion that all cops were thieves, but Simone had taken the joke seriously. If the law stopped you, Don Michele added, a Rolex was the first thing they'd notice before they started asking serious questions.

'Make out you're a poor bastard, just like them, Simò, or be ready to blast the fuckers.'

03.23.

Seven minutes to rendezvous.

The farmhouse was unlit, but that was normal for a safe house when no one was hiding there. He boosted the magnification, concentrating on the windowpanes. If there were coppers in the vicinity, they'd be well hidden, but they wouldn't be able to cover every angle. He went from window to window, but there were no reflections, nothing suspicious, no one to be seen . . .

No one?

Where were the donkeys?

A ton and a half of stuff coming in, there should have been half a dozen men out there, waiting to offload it into the van. He scanned the field to the left of the farmhouse. It was lying fallow, half a dozen sheep to crop the grass. If the labourers were donkeys, those sheep were lawnmowers. So where was the van? The field was empty, except for the stacks of straw, already drenched with petrol, he imagined.

03.28.

Two minutes to go . . .

Then he heard it, felt it almost, as if the air was changing in consistency. The distant rumble took on a mechanical thrum as it homed in on the landing place. He glanced back down at the farm and the field. He'd been distracted by the noise in the sky, hadn't seen the fires being lit. There were five of them forming a blazing circle, fifty or sixty metres in diameter.

It would have needed five men to light those fires on cue.

The noise was steady now, a regular thumping. Any kid who'd seen a film could tell you what was making that racket. He could hear it, though he still couldn't see it. The pilot was flying without navigation lights, the cockpit dark as the big bird swooped in on the circle of bonfires down in the plain between the ridge and the lake.

Then the noise changed somehow, becoming syncopated, yet out of sync, as if the engine had whooping cough. He took no notice, too busy watching as the Agusta Koala appeared in stark silhouette against the flames, rearing back sharply, then settling down on its landing skis in the centre of the circle. Then men came running out from behind the farm buildings.

Too many men . . .

As the rotor blades slowed down, he heard the other noise more distinctly.

He swung the binoculars upwards, saw it hovering above the black Koala. It, too, was painted black, but it was bigger, a bug-like military helicopter with white letters written on the flank: *CARABINIERI.* They were blocking any attempt at an emergency take off, the men on the ground moving in fast. Arc lights flashed on, and he saw the scene in startling clarity. Armed *carabinieri* closing in, machine-guns aimed at the cockpit, warning the pilot and his mate that it was useless to try and escape.

Don Michele had just lost a helicopter, a ton and a half of coke, a van, some cars, two pilots and half a dozen soldiers.

Jesus! What were you supposed to tell him?

Simone slid back down the slope on the seat of his pants, ran to the car.

He tried to drive back slowly to Catanzaro, but it was hard to stop his foot from pressing the accelerator down to the floor.

TWO

Sibillines National Park, Umbria.

Sebastiano Cangio reached for his binoculars.

It was a thrill to be up on Mount Coscerno again. The sky was clear, a myriad stars, the land below so dark, so quiet, you could almost hear the grass grow. His heart was pumping with excitement. He had started work at midday, finished the shift at nine o'clock, but he wouldn't be going home just yet. This was the time he liked the best, the witching hour, when the creatures of the night came out to play.

Thank God for Marzio, he thought.

Marzio Diamante was his partner at the ranger station. Marzio had a wife and a family – two grown-up daughters, both married, and his first grandchild, baby Matteo. Marzio wasn't one to spend his nights out on the mountainside getting cold. He was happy to let Cangio do the late shift. Marzio would be roasting chestnuts over a log fire in the kitchen, washing them down with a glass of Montefalco red.

One glass? More like three or four.

Cangio focused his night-glasses and began to search the steep slope on the other side of the gorge.

The underground den was over to the left in the lee of a thorn bush, but he knew they would have abandoned it for the summer. Like everyone else, they drifted off on holiday when the weather was hot, moving on to higher ground, looking for a change of scene and diet. Now, with autumn coming on, and another breeding season to look forward to, he wasn't sure whether the female would reclaim the old den or go looking for a new one somewhere else. It would all depend on how the pack had fared over the summer.

He had followed the breeding pair through the previous spring, seen the four blind pups – all male – crawl out of the den one night, watched in wonder as they started to walk within a few days, then run and play at rough and tumble, just like kids growing up in a normal family, and then . . .

Then he had gone and got himself shot.

Well, no, he thought, before getting shot he had taken Loredana up there one night. First, he had shown her the pups through his binoculars, and then they had made love on the canvas on which he was lying at that very moment. He had been on convalescent leave for more than three months, but now the wound had healed and he was back at work, getting slowly into the rhythm of an eight- or twelve-hour day, patrolling the forests and the mountains, keeping an eye on the tourists and the wildlife.

He was dying to see the wolves again.

He shifted the night-glasses to the east, studying the granite boulder outcrop that formed a solid bump against the star-spattered sky. That clump of rocks provided a perfect vantage point. From there you could see in three directions down the mountainside. If anything moved on the slopes below, the scout would see it, let out a low howl and call the others to join the hunt.

Nothing was happening over there.

Above his head, something let out a squeal. A bird or a bat, maybe. That was the good thing about Mount Coscerno. There was no lack of food. Down in the valley there were cats, dogs and sheep. Wild boar, porcupine and hedgehogs lived in the woods on the lower slopes above the river, while deer, goats, hares, rabbits and all the birds you could possibly imagine – from sparrows to sparrowhawks – lived on the upper slopes of Mount Coscerno. Just the day before, he had spotted a pair of golden eagles riding the air currents high above the plain of Castelluccio . . .

Something moved beyond his left eye.

He shifted the night-glasses, and began to count.

One, two, three, four, moving in order of size or rank, he hadn't yet worked it out.

The theory was that they were hierarchical creatures, but on-site observation often told a different story, almost as if each one had a distinct personality which defined their place in the pecking order, depending on what activity they were involved in. If one was sick, it led the way, setting the pace for the ones behind. The last of the group disappeared from sight – there must have been a sharp dip in the ground – and he started counting again as the first dark shadow emerged from the blackness, each one a stark silhouette with bright yellow eyes against the fluorescent green field of the background. Night scopes were useful, OK, but the colours were lurid.

Four, five, six, seven . . . Seven!

He almost let out a shout. Seven of the group had survived. Just as he had survived.

And one had died, just as he might have died if that bullet had cut through an artery.

He watched them cross the face of the mountain.

They gradually picked up momentum as they approached the old den, cantering over the last fifty metres, the breeding female in the lead, taking them home, her mate tucked in behind her tail, the three surving pups – pups no longer – with the rolling gait and independent air of increasing maturity, the two older cubs that had stayed with the pack from the previous season bringing up the rear.

Seeing them like this, it was hard to think of them as a 'pack'.

The word sounded savage and vicious, while they were a disciplined, ordered family, each one knowing its role and its place. The female nursed and guarded the young cubs while the male and the older cubs went out hunting. The parents had taken turns feeding the little ones, chewing meat to a pulp, then regurgitating it for the pups to feed on.

Wow! he thought again.

They halted outside the den, waited for the female to sniff around, then enter.

Then the six males, the father and two generations of sons, raised their muzzles to the moon and began to wail like a heavenly choir.

Ooooo0OoooooooOoooooo!

Sebastiano Cangio felt like wailing along with them.

THREE

Catanzaro, Calabria.

The wide-screen TV was tuned to Sky News.

The don must have known what was coming 'cause he told them all to shut the fuck up.

'Gimme a piece of *that*!' he said, aiming the remote control at the blonde goddess reading the midday news, boosting the volume. 'Which whorehouse do they find them in? It ain't one of ours, I can tell you. OK now, here we go.'

Guatemala, the printout said. Some place with a mouthful of a name. A jungle scene. A village of shabby bamboo huts.

'The police are cracking down on local drugs lords,' the blonde was saying. 'Four tons of unprocessed cocaine were destroyed in this raid alone.'

The pictures on the screen showed paramilitary police with flamethrowers gutting the village laboratory, burning the crop, prisoners being marched away, their hands tied behind their backs.

Don Michele pressed the button and the picture disappeared.

He cursed for a full minute – the cops, their wives, their kids – the peasant coming out in him, the part he usually kept well hidden, the inherited dirt beneath his manicured fingernails showing through.

He was usually so calm, it stunned them into silence.

'The paramilitaries in Guatemala have wrecked seventeen jungle factories in the last few days. Most of the top men out in the field have been arrested. Some of that stuff was meant for us. I can cover the emergency for a couple of months, then we'll need to stock up on the open market – whatever the fucking price. What we need now,' he said, looking from one man to the next, 'is a solid long-term strategy.'

He was thinking out loud, not expecting anyone to say a word.

Simone Candelora counted to three before he opened his mouth, and while he counted a phrase kept hammering through his brain, a phrase that Julius Caesar was supposed to have said when he led his army across the River Rubicon and started the war against the Senate which would turn him into a legend.

Alea iacta est.

The die is cast, there's no going back.

Candelora took a deep breath. 'What if we forget South America, Don Michè?' he said. 'Maybe there's a better source.'

Don Michele let out a snort of laughter. 'Just listen to the prof!' he said. Then he turned to the others, said, 'Why didn't you lot go to fucking university?'

The others started to laugh, as if the idea was stupid, and what a joke the boss had cracked, but the don cut through the noise. 'What have you got in mind, Simò?'

Simone Candelora was the youngest man in the room, the newest addition to the clan. He stared back at Don Michele for a moment, and he didn't back down.

Alea iacta est.

'Asia,' Candelora said. 'That's what I've been thinking.'

The don didn't move a muscle. 'You know the place?' he said at last.

Maybe the others were taking bets, because the don turned round and told them all to shut it. Everyone knew that the kid had been to college. He had a doctorate in agronomy, whatever that was. But Asia? Come on.

'I know it well,' Simone said. 'Last time I was out there for seven months. Thailand, Vietnam, Laos. All the way to the Pacific coast—'

'Doing what?' someone challenged him.

Don Michele wasn't having it. He held up his hand for silence. Then he asked the same thing. 'What were you doing out there?'

'Studying the layout, Don Michè. The university gave me a travel grant. It's the promised land out there, rich and fertile, jungle everywhere. It's got everything you need. It's hot, it rains a lot, and coppers are thin on the ground.' He held Don Michele's gaze for a moment. 'They grow the stuff all right, but they don't know how to move it around.'

The don lit a thin cheroot, blew a stream of smoke into the air. 'Asia? OK,' he said, 'that's one end of the chain. But where are you thinking of joining up the links?'

Simone paused for a moment. He could almost hear the others drawing breath.

Alea iacta est.

'What about Umbria, Don Michè? You've got the connections, and the place has quietened down now. It's still the perfect place to run an operation, boss.'

He had tacked that 'boss' on the end, and was relieved to see the effect it had.

Don Michele hid a smile by sucking long and hard on his cheroot.

Simone knew what had happened in Umbria six months before. Don Michele had tried to move in on the earthquake reconstruction, the ocean of cash that was leaking from the European Commission and the International Monetary Fund. Then his men up there had gone and cocked it up.

Don Michele pulled a face, the corners of his mouth turning down. 'Umbria? What the fuck are we gonna do up there? Ettore's handling the distribution, but it's small time, nothing special. He's been keeping an eye on that ranger, too.' More smoke came out, and a sigh came with it. 'When things cool off, he'll get what's coming to him.'

Simone Candelora knew who the don was talking about. One of the others had told him about the debacle in Umbria. A right disaster by all accounts, and all because of some nosey park ranger.

'Yogi Bear?' Simone said lightly, joking, but with an edge. 'We can settle with him any time you say, Don Michè—'

'Not now,' Don Michele warned, his finger raised. 'That

Cangio's a nobody, more dangerous dead than alive. More useful living. We leave him to the *carabinieri* for the time being. Once he's testified against that general of theirs, they won't give a flyin' fuck what happens to Cangio. In the meantime, we get on with business.'

'That's just what I had in mind.'

'What *have* you got in mind precisely, Simò?'

'Something quiet. Something small, though it could get bigger. Someone in trouble, you know what I mean, a decent company, a fair name, but the banks and debtors are sucking it dry. A one-man business. The owner's got to be clean, of course, no track record. Clean as a brand new plate-glass window. Then we move in.'

Don Michele tugged on his cheroot. 'And where do we find this holy sucker?'

'I've got banking contacts, Don Michè. I can find him.'

Don Michele stubbed the cheroot and stood up, bringing the meeting to an end.

He placed his hand on Simone's shoulder as they all filed out of the room. 'I fancy a tasty slice of fish, Simò. You ever been to Mamma Rosa's out on the coast road? *Strangolapreti alle vongole*, then swordfish steak with fresh dill? We can talk some more about this scheme of yours over lunch.'

The others were watching as he climbed into the car with Don Michele. Even if they'd never heard the expression, they were learning what it meant now by bitter experience.

Alea iacta est . . .

The dice were rolling his way.

FOUR

A town in Umbria.

It was ten past nine when he got to the bank.

The secretary glanced up at him, and let out a sigh. 'I'm sorry, *Signor* Marra,' she said, 'the finance manager has a busy day ahead of him, and *Signor* B . . . well, another gentleman was waiting. I'm sure he'll see you as soon as he's free. Would you care to take a seat?'

What else could he do?

Could you bite the hand you hoped was going to feed you?

He sat down, and examined his Eberhard watch. The Chrono 4 would have to go if nothing came of this meeting. That would give him breathing space for . . . what? A week, ten days at the most. The Jag had gone already, traded in for a bit of cash and a clapped-out Mondeo. The house was up for sale, but the bottom had fallen out of the property market, so it was either give it away or forget about it. For the moment, he was living off his undeclared earnings. If the tax people ever caught up with him on that score, he'd be doing time.

It was the fourth time he'd been there that month.

The first time, he had tried anger, but that hadn't worked. He'd given logic a go the time after that, and he'd been forced to face the fact that the bank was more logical and far less forgiving than he had been led to believe. On the last occasion, he had tried to appeal to the finance manager's sense of civic pride, only to be told that the bank had been absorbed by a big city bank which was part of a national banking group which had just merged with a larger European holding, and that he, Arnaldo Capaldi, humble finance manager of the local branch bank, was the lowliest of the low in a very long line of obedient servants who could do very little to help Antonio Marra.

As Capaldi had told him the last time: you can't mortgage what you haven't got.

'Would you care for a coffee?' the secretary asked him.

Once, he might have said no, but things had changed. Nowadays, he never said no when anything was free. 'Thanks,' he said. 'Two sugars. No, make that three.'

He was finishing his coffee when the door opened, and Gianni Borlotti came creeping out of the finance manager's office like a condemned man going to the whipping post, head down, back bent, his face like one of those Smiley stickers with the lips turned down.

'Antonio!' Borlotti exclaimed, and his face lit up with a brittle Hollywood grin.

Antonio Marra jumped up, and forced an even brighter smile. 'Ciao, Gianni. How are things?'

'Things are . . . you know. Fine, just fine,' Borlotti managed to say, his bobbing Adam's apple giving him away. 'What about you, Antò?'

Antonio Marra was spared the same embarrassing lie. The finance manager's door opened, and a wagging finger inviting him to step inside. 'See you, Gianni,' Marra said, and turned away. It was a bit like avoiding hot grease by jumping into boiling vegetable oil.

'*Signor* Marra,' the finance manager said, a bright smile on his face today, his hand held out in unexpected greeting, 'I am pleased to say that we have been approached by a potential, and very wealthy, investor. I have his prospectus here, and I'll be happy to go over the details with you. I believe that you'd do well to consider the proposal.'

'Can I speak with *Signor* Candelora?'

'You've got him.'

The voice at the other end of the phone went from brisk to pure honey.

'It's me *Signor* Candelora, Arnaldo Capaldi. From the bank in Umbria. I do hope the weather's nice down where you . . .'

'Listen, Capaldi, you don't give a dried shit what the weather's like in Calabria, and I'm not going to waste time telling you. Let's cut out the two-old-ladies crap, and get straight down to business. Have you got news for me?'

Capaldi sounded a bit less sure of himself. At least he'd stopped licking arse. 'I certainly have, *Signor* Candelora. I doubt that you'd find a better one than this. The company is just perfect. He's the man you're looking for.'

'He's got a spotless sheet?'

'Like a newborn babe's.'

Candelora sank back on the pillow, pushed aside the books he'd been consulting. *The Michelin Guide to Umbria. The Annual Economic Report on the State of Central Italy. Renewal and Expansion in Umbria after the Earthquake.*

'Tell me more, Capaldi. The details. Annual turnover, the size of the plant, number of employees, the type of product that we're dealing with, the debts and the mortgages, the whole works.'

In ten minutes, Capaldi had given him the long and the short of it. Some shady dealing, nothing proven, nothing criminal, but that was par for the course. All that was missing was the size of the owner's shoes and underpants, the altitude and latitude of his factory.

It was time to give the dog his bone.

'You're on the ball, Capaldi. Now, what else was there? Oh yeah, your cut . . . The cash will start to flow once this newborn babe has signed on the dotted line. Give me a blow as soon as the deal's set up, OK. I'll be up there like a shot . . . Oh yeah, thanks, and the same to you. Have a nice day.'

Candelora snapped the phone shut, tapped it gently against his teeth.

He put the phone down, opened the silver snuffbox, poured a healthy measure onto the protective glass of the bedside table, chopped and divided it with his platinum card, then took the two lines of coke, one in each nostril.

He was already buzzing, but a bit more focus always helped. He couldn't wait to tell Don Michele that the plan was off the ground, that they would soon be the majority shareholder in a small company in the Sibillines National Park.

An hour ago Marra Truffles had been dead on its feet.

Now, it was ready to fly.

FIVE

Catanzaro, Calabria.

D on Michele held up the jar, and read the yellow label. 'Are we going into the food industry now, Simò?'

Simone Candelora felt beads of sweat erupt out on his brow.

'Just untwist the cap, Don Michè, then tell me what you think.'

The don narrowed his eyes and stared at him. 'If you're pissing me about . . .' he warned, as he opened the jar, held it to his nose, and inhaled. 'Truffles?'

'Top wedge, Don Michè. They export them all over the world

as pastes and sauces. The USA, Europe, the Middle East, Australia. And that distinctive aroma? The sniffer dogs are trained to ignore it when they're working at customs.' He took another identical jar from his pocket, untwisted the lid and handed it to the don. 'Now, try this one.'

Don Michele rolled his eyes, his patience running thin.

'Truffle sauce, same brand,' the boss confirmed with a sniff and a growl.

'Maybe yes, but maybe no,' Candelora said. 'Let's see what this item here can tell us.'

He took a plastic wallet from his inside pocket, removed a glass ampoule of clear liquid, tore two small sheets of paper from the booklet and lay them down on the desk. He took a smear of sauce from one jar with one square of paper, and then did the same with the other jar and the second piece of paper.

'Is this a fucking chemistry lesson, Simò?'

Simone Candelora cracked the end of the ampoule and let a few drops of liquid fall on the two pieces of paper smeared with truffle sauce. Inside ten seconds, one of the papers turned blue.

He handed the instruction leaflet to the don.

'*Quick Home Coca Test,*' Don Michele read.

'They sell these kits in the States so parents can check on their delinquent kids. This jar here,' Simone Candelora pointed, 'is fifty per cent pure.'

'*Marra Truffles*?' the boss said, reading the label carefully now. 'Tell me more.'

'Antonio Marra, sole owner and regular fuck-up. Inherited a truffle reserve and the family business. His father started processing truffles, trying to export them – wanted to compete with the local big boys, but died before he got there. The only son comes along and the company goes bottom up. He's a regular spender – cars, women, gambling – so he starts borrowing. He's just about hanging on by the skin of his dick.'

That made Don Michele laugh. 'Is he clean, this truffle merchant? Will he play along?'

Simone Candelora couldn't keep a straight face. He'd checked the Chamber of Commerce, the local and regional trade associations, the public statements of accounts.

'No problem, Don Michè,' Simone assured him. 'He's perfect.

Speeding fines apart, he's got a clean sheet. What's even better, he's up to his eyes in solid debt.'

Don Michele poked his finger into the jar that had tested positive, then sucked on his finger, closing his eyes for a moment or two, before he opened them wide.

'Help him, Simò,' he said. 'Help him.'

SIX

Sibillines National Park, Umbria.

'Two months in Todi?'

'They need an assistant manager to tide them over. They've got the staff, but they don't know how a shop works. It's only for a couple of months, Seb. Todi's seventy kilometres away. It isn't in Alaska.'

'I thought you weren't interested in a career?'

Lori smiled at that. 'A career? With a supermarket chain? There's no such thing, but it is a job and I need it. I can't depend on you to feed me always, can I? If they start sacking people, I don't intend to be on the list. I'd *like* to think that they need me.'

'I need you,' Cangio said.

Loredana Salvini was unlike any woman he had met in London.

She wasn't pushy, she wasn't ambitious. She had a healthy appetite in every sense of the word, a bit of puppy fat that drove him wild. They'd been together eight months now, and had managed not to argue. She had nursed him in the hospital, moved in with him when the doctors let him out. She had nursed him, cooked for him, made love to him and treated him like a friend. And now she was going to Todi?

He turned towards her, laid his hands on her shoulders, held her down on the bed.

'I won't let you get away,' he said, nuzzling between her breasts.

'Is that so?' she said. 'What do you need me for? Since you've been back on your feet, I don't even get to hand out the painkillers.

You don't need anyone, Seb. A pair of binoculars, a jeep and the park, and your life's complete.' She raised her head from the pillow, looked straight into his eyes. 'Did I forget something there? Oh, yeah, the wolves, naturally.'

Was this tale about Todi true? Had they asked her, or had she asked them? Was she taking a break from him, or was she putting him to the test? Then again, maybe she was putting herself to the test, seeing whether she could live without him.

He didn't like the idea, that went without saying. Todi wasn't Alaska, but it was a long way away, too far to drive there and back every day, and a lot of things could happen to two people in two months.

Things had changed between them, there was no denying it, and it had all started with the 'Ndrangheta and General Corsini. She'd taken time off work after he had been shot, ready and willing to do whatever needed to be done. Sitting by his bed, running errands, paying his bills, holding his hand when the doctors took him off the morphine drip and the pain kicked in.

He didn't like the idea of being without Loredana.

'I thought that you might run away to London again,' she had confessed one day. 'I mean to say, Seb, they tried to kill you, didn't they? They could try again. And if you stay here . . .'

'I don't intend to run,' he had told her. 'Ever again.'

'We could leave Umbria, go somewhere quieter.'

Quieter than Umbria?

He had put his hand over her mouth.

'Look at me, Lori,' he had said, seeing the fear in her eyes. 'Listen to me. I'm not going anywhere. This is where I live. This is where I intend to stay. I'm not leaving or running away.'

Now, the shoe was on the other foot. She was going away. She was running scared for her job. She was going to Todi. OK, in two months she'd be back, but would things still be the same between them?

He held her wrists, raised her arms, and pushed himself inside of her.

She let out a cry of surprise; there was fear in it, pleasure, too.

She had turned up out of nowhere; she could disappear the same way.

He made love to her, hard and passionately, but there was no tenderness in it.

Like a wolf, he thought, a wolf on the run.

A wolf that knows that time is running out.

It's now, or never.

Now, or never again.

The sense of danger excited him.

But there was no running away from danger.

If you ran, you were lost.

The next day, Lori went to Todi.

SEVEN

Sibillines National Park, Umbria.

'What do you mean, no good?'

'That is *not* what I said, Antonio. Not *positive.* That's what I said.'

As usual, the tarot cards were laid out on the kitchen table in the form of a cross.

As usual, Maria Gatti was sitting there in the flickering light, staring at him, her long fingernails petting the cards, making scratching noises on the wooden tabletop.

Talk about a witch! Dyed-black hair, the grey roots showing through. Black mascara, black nail varnish, blue and red tattoos on her chest and shoulders, and that silver ring stuck in her nose. Her eyes stared out at him from deep dark caverns caked with eyeliner. It was like peering into a well, her eyes two points of light far away in the darkness.

'They look . . . hm . . . real negative to me.'

Antonio Marra was sitting in Maria Gatti's kitchen, the room lit only by candles.

Her spirits had led her to the farmhouse in the woods, she claimed, the spirits of the dead, though everyone knew that she'd inherited the place from her mother. He hated going up there at night, and not just because of the dead souls she said had made their home with her. It was the wolves he was frightened of, the place was so isolated. The wolves had never bothered her, she said, calling them her 'sisters of the night', but where did that leave him?

As a rule, he got her to stop by the factory after the workers had all gone home.

Today, though, he'd been in a hurry to see her.

The deal had gone through, the finance manager telling him his credit problems were solved, something about moving forward into a new era of prosperity and tranquillity. Capaldi's exact words: 'The bank will be honoured to meet your every need.'

And now Maria Gatti was telling him that the tarot cards said no?

He ought to tell her this was the end.

When things had been black, it had done no harm to know just how black things really were. But now? What the fuck was he doing here? Why had he asked her to read the cards for him? He hated that fucking kitchen, the mouldy smell of fry-ups and goat's cheese. The only thing the kitchen had going for it was the lack of cats. She kept them away from the food, and there were no photos or stuffed felines to be seen in there, unlike the rest of the house.

To think that he'd let her creep into his bed a few years back made his skin crawl.

Jesus, had he been desperate!

And he'd come so full of hope and light, good fortune shining on him! He'd wanted to brag a bit. He'd wanted her to confirm it, to tell him that she saw it in the stars. And what had she done? She turned over the cards and pulled a fucking face – the Hanging Man, the Moon with the howling dog and the snarling wolf, then the Tower.

The worst of the worst.

'Do you know these people?' Maria had asked him, resting her clammy, cold hand on his, digging her nails into his skin, not letting go of him.

'Who they are, you mean?' he'd said. 'Who the fuck cares! OK, I've been through some tough times. They know I need hard cash to get things back on the rails. They're happy to invest, proud to be a part of Marra Truffles.'

The more he talked, the angrier he got.

With himself.

Why waste time with the likes of Maria Gatti?

In the end, he'd told her.

'My dear Maria, I hate to say this, love, but the cards have got it wrong.'

Maria Gatti had raised those lamps and turned her dark orbs on him.

'Have they ever been wrong before, Antò?'

When he finally got out of there, he cursed himself for wasting time and the bag of truffles he'd given her instead of paying cash. Still, he thought, as he climbed into the old Mondeo, he could afford to be generous now.

Generous with himself, too. Yeah, why not?

He'd call in at the Porsche dealership in Foligno before he went home and have a look at that near-new midnight blue 911 Turbo they had up on display. What a way to celebrate the comeback of Marra Truffles!

The name on the bank draft belonged to an investor from the south with an advanced degree in agronomy, whatever that might be. *Simone Candelora . . .*

He liked the sound of the name, and liked the healthy bank balance even better. The old nursery rhyme came into his head: *'Con la Madonna candelora dall'inverno semo fora.'*

When Our Lady of the Candles comes . . .

What was the date of the *candelora*, the middle of March? It meant the end of the dark days of winter, and forty days to the start of spring. Simone Candelora had brought him more candles than he could have hoped for.

Now there'd be some bright lights for a change.

If he put his foot down, he could be in Foligno before the dealership closed.

EIGHT

Sibillines National Park, Umbria.

'These folks are nutters, Cangio.'

Marzio Diamante, the senior ranger, was something of a nutter himself. As they were changing shifts at two o'clock, Marzio had told him to take a look at the abandoned church on the road out to Poggiodomo.

'I stopped off there this morning,' Marzio had said. 'A sect's been messing about in the chapel if you ask me. See what you make of it.'

There was a park to look after, maintenance work that needing doing, reports of poachers out near Roccaporena, wild boar wrecking gardens and allotments down by the river, and Marzio wanted him to drive up to Poggiodomo and take a look at an abandoned church.

He had been to Roccaporena, taken the farmer's statement, and then he had made the circuit, stopping off at Poggiodomo on the way back to keep Marzio happy.

He parked on the track, and walked towards the building.

The church looked like a cowshed. If not for the tourist information sign, no one would ever have thought of stopping there. And yet, someone had been there. The heavy door had been kicked in, the lock and the bolt hanging loose, revealing a low barrel-vaulted chamber that might have held a dozen people at the most. Though the church was named after San Pancrazio in the regional guidebook, local people still called it the Sacred Image.

If there had ever been a sacred image, it was long gone.

Could you still call it a church?

All that remained were four crumbling walls and a primitive fresco of the Virgin Mary which thieves had never judged worth stealing over the centuries.

There was no saying no to Marzio, that was the trouble. Talk about stubborn. When he got something fixed in his head, there was no shaking it out again.

He clambered over the rubble, lit his torch, then stepped inside the hovel.

It was dark in there. Spooky, Marzio would have said. The roof was ready to come down; it was sagging badly on one side. It would fall down too, sooner or later, because no one was going to pay to restore a forgotten country chapel that hadn't been used for centuries.

There was a circle of stones on the ground, bits of burnt wood and dry ash.

He picked up one of the stones, sniffed it and dropped it back inside the circle.

Sometimes these places were used by tourists, walkers, boy scouts, sometimes tramps; people looking for a free roof over their heads for a night without any mod cons, like a bathroom or a toilet.

Sometimes you found the evidence smeared on the walls.

Have a look at the altar stone, Marzio had told him.

It was dry inside the chapel, warm. There was nothing sinister about the place, though Marzio saw the sinister everywhere. He had visions of people dancing naked beneath the stars, orgies by candlelight, witches whispering magic formulas, conjuring up ghosts, sacrificing beautiful virgins on desecrated altars.

Wishful thinking, Cangio thought.

A bit like him and London. Marzio couldn't get over the fact that he hated the place.

Marzio would have given his right arm to live and work in a big city. Like a lot of people born in the country, Marzio hated the land, hated his job, though he was conscientious about it. He would hang on, doing his duty, no doubt, until he was pensionable.

'You should go back to London,' Marzio had said one day. It wasn't that he wanted to be shut of him. He hadn't meant to offend. It was just his way of saying things. Marzio would never imagine that you might take it badly. 'After all the bloody fuss you caused, you'd be a celebrity in England now.'

Cangio moved towards the altar, pointing his flashlight, holding it steady.

Six-six-six, Marzio had said. That's the Devil's symbol, they say.

He played the light all over the altar-stone, top, front, back and sides. There were squiggles and scratches, nothing he could make much sense of, apart from a heart done in charcoal around the initials *PV + AT*.

What should he tell Marzio?

Tell him the truth, obviously.

Someone had been roasting sausages over an open fire in the church of San Pancrazio.

What difference did it make? Orgy or sausages? Even if you caught these people, nothing would ever come of it. Marzio was right about one thing, though. If they took their clothes off in that place, they really *were* nutters. With all the rats, they'd catch a dose of leptospirosis.

He left the chapel, retraced his steps, jumped into the Land Rover and swung it around.

His shift was nearly over. Back to the ranger station, pick up the Fiat 500, and then spend an hour or two watching the wolves.

Tomorrow he'd tell Marzio what he hadn't found.

NINE

Umbria, Central Italy.

He knew he was dreaming.

Lori's silhouette was moving on the ground glass screen, raising her arms as she washed her hair and soaped her breasts inside the shower. Only the splashing sound of cascading water was missing.

It was like a silent movie, action only, a hollow vision, nothing more.

She'd been in Todi two weeks now, and every morning he woke up in the middle of the same dream: Lori taking a shower . . .

He was like one of those amputees who can't get used to the

idea that an arm or a leg has gone forever, who still feel the itch of a missing limb.

Was that how he missed her?

He woke up every morning in the grip of a desire to hold her, to touch her, and then a cold, metallic voice would sound in his head as the dream drew towards its close.

Just a couple of months, Seb. A couple of months.

The first day, he had phoned her a dozen times. The second day, half as often. It was exponential. Each day they seemed to have less to say to each other, their worlds so far apart. The last few days, it had just been text messages, and they were getting shorter and shorter.

Are you OK?

Busy.

He threw off the bedclothes, swung his leg out of bed and pain bit into his thigh. The gunshot wound was taking time to heal, and Lori had left him to his fate. Rain today, he thought, and maybe thunder. It was better than a barometer, though the weather forecast the night before had been quite promising. If legs could speak, he knew what it would tell him.

Stay in bed, Seb, make the most of your free morn—

His telephone trilled like a grasshopper, vibrating and shifting on the bedside table.

He groaned again, picked it up, hoping it was Lori.

'Cangio? Sustrico here.'

Tonino Sustrico, commanding officer of the *carabinieri* in Spoleto, had visited him in hospital and taken his statement regarding the shooting that was causing the pain in his thigh, clearly embarrassed by the fact that a fellow *carabiniere* had nearly let Seb Cangio bleed to death. Sustrico had come back more than once to see how he was getting on.

'More papers to sign?' Cangio asked him.

The *carabinieri* general who had put Cangio's life at risk would soon be going on trial.

'It's nothing to do with General Corsini,' Sustrico said brusquely, and then he went quiet.

'So what is this? An early wake-up call?'

'There's something I want you to see,' the *carabiniere* said at last.

'Do you want me to come into town this morning?'

'I want you to meet me at the Vallo di Nera turn-off in fifteen minutes.'

The phone went dead before Cangio could ask him why.

Cangio rode north in the Fiat 500.

There was no heating in the tiny old car which Lori's dad had loaned him.

The sun was coming up, promising another Indian summer day. Its rays were like a golden crown above the dark hump of Mount Coscerno, but it was freezing cold down in the valley. A light coating of October frost glistened off the black tarmac surface, so he had to take it easy. The Valnerina road was dangerous at any time of the year, weaving like a snake through the valley as it followed the winding course of the River Nera.

Sustrico was alone in a patrol car at the Vallo di Nera turn-off, his fingers drumming on the steering wheel. As Cangio pulled in behind the midnight blue Alfa Romeo 159, the *carabiniere* threw open the passenger door. The message was clear. Cangio cut the motor, removed the ignition key and climbed in beside the *brigadiere*.

'What's all the mystery about?' he asked.

Sustrico fired up the engine and pulled away sharply. 'A body's been found in the woods above Vallo di Nera,' he said. 'Two of my officers were out on night patrol, so I sent them up there immediately. Just before I called you, they'd called me back.'

Cangio felt his blood go cold. A death in the national park was the last thing he wanted to hear about. There had been too many dead bodies in the park in the recent past.

Sustrico took a bend too wide and the big car skidded on the gravel.

'I thought the body might be yours,' the *carabiniere* said.

Cangio struggled to make sense of what he was hearing. 'Mine?'

'I mean to say, if you've been shot once . . .'

Did that make sense to Sustrico? If there was a body in the woods, it had to be Cangio's?

'You phoned to check if I was alive or dead?'

'In the first instance, yes. You know this area better than most people.' Sustrico cleared his throat. 'And, well . . . the body will need to be identified.'

Cangio ran through the possibilities in silence. There were lots of ways to die in a national park. Poachers sometimes shot each other by mistake. People fell off mountain bikes, slipped off cliffs, capsized canoes, or waded out of their depth while fishing for trout. Sometimes people just got lost in the woods and there was no one to report them missing – old age pensioners who went out looking for mushrooms and never came back. It happened more frequently than people might imagine. In the wild, if something went wrong, you were on your own.

'Where was the body found?'

'Somewhere up there,' Sustrico said, pointing his finger at the wood-covered mountain that loomed ahead of them. 'What do they call it? Coscerno?'

'Coscerno's the next one in the range, *brigadiere*. This is Mount Bacugno.'

The *carabiniere* didn't have the foggiest idea where he was. He probably hadn't been into the mountains for months or years. Maybe never. As the Alfa raced into the shadow of the cliffs, he fumbled with the headlights. The sun wouldn't reach that side of the mountain for hours yet. Less than a kilometre beyond the town, the road rose sharply. As they rounded a bend, flashing red-and-blue lights came into sight.

Sustrico accelerated with a skid on the loose gravel.

Another Alfa 159 with *Carabinieri* written on the flank in white letters was blocking the road, its roof lights flashing on and off. Sustrico braked, got out of the car, and cupped his gloved hands to his mouth. 'Pulenti!' he shouted.

A voice called back, telling him to wait by the car, and a couple of minutes later a bald, middle-aged *carabiniere* came tumbling out of the bushes without his cap.

'*Brigadiere!*' he said, not coming to attention, but touching his forehead with two joined fingers.

'Report,' Sustrico commanded.

'We've got some witnesses, sir.'

'Well, that's a relief!' Sustrico breathed out like a locomotive letting off steam. 'Who are they?'

'Two men and a dog, sir.'

Antonio Marra was on his way to work when the action started.

On the zigzag stretch of road between Sant'Anatolia and Vallo di Nera, a car with flashing roof lights came roaring up behind him, easing off just three or four metres short of his bumper, as he went into the sharp bend where the river horseshoed back on itself and the road was forced to do the same.

'Fucking *carabinieri*!' he cursed.

Just the sight of the uniform or a patrol car would bring him out in a cold sweat. They'd already done him twice for speeding. That was the trouble with the Porsche. It attracted cops like flies to a dog turd.

'Fuck, fuck, fuck!'

He wanted to slow down, wanted to stop, but the *carabinieri* wouldn't let him. They stayed right behind him, flashing their headlights and forcing him to up his speed. They'd be filming his car, noting the license plate, recording everything.

Jesus, they were making him go faster!

He came out of the bend, hit the straight and indicated right to show that he was going to stop, and what did they do? They went flying past, ignoring him totally. As he picked up speed again, he saw the Alfa, a kilometre ahead, signal right, then head off in the direction of Vallo di Nera.

'Hope you die, bastards!' he said out loud.

As he turned into Marra Truffles, he wiped the sweat off his brow.

Two men were waiting in the clearing, standing shoulder to shoulder like Siamese twins. One of them was smoking a cigarette. A tawny-coloured dachshund had made itself comfortable on a pile of leaves at their feet and seemed to be fast asleep.

Cangio had seen them occasionally in the woods above Vallo di Nera, always together, and always with the same little sausage dog. Marzio Diamante, the senior ranger, had told him who they were, but he couldn't recall their names.

Both men were staring at something on the far side of the clearing.

Cangio looked that way and saw a uniform and badge that he recognised – a crown, a golden eagle and the motto: *Pro Natura Opus et Vigilantia*. The corpse appeared to be sitting on the ground, arms by its sides, the palms face upwards, legs stretched out in front of the torso, the back propped up against a tree.

Cangio's stomach rolled.

The head was missing—

'Marzio?' he managed to say.

'Marzio Diamante,' Sustrico confirmed.

'Jesus holy Christ . . .'

Cangio stared at the mess of blood on the shoulders and chest, the shredded fibres where the throat had been. He couldn't breathe, couldn't think, couldn't look. He turned away: the severed head was peeping out of the undergrowth a metre away, both eyes wide open, the mouth a gaping—

He gagged hard, clamping his hand to his mouth.

'. . . point-blank range,' Sustrico was saying. 'Probably a sawn-off twelve-bore.'

What had Marzio been doing there?

'If you're on patrol and you run into trouble,' Marzio had always told him, 'call me, the police and the *carabinieri*.' That was the standard procedure, especially with poachers. Poachers were armed as a rule, which made them dangerous.

Why hadn't Marzio phoned?

An answer leapt to mind straight off: poaching didn't come into it.

Sustrico's voice sliced through his thoughts. He was talking to the witnesses.

'What were you two doing here?' Sustrico asked them.

'It's our job, *brigadiere*. We're *cavatori*.' One of the men held up a strange tool like a long walking stick with a two-pronged fork welded to the bottom end.

'*Cavatori?*' Sustrico echoed.

'Diggers,' Cangio explained. 'Hunting for truffles.'

'Names?' Sustrico snapped.

'Pastore, *brigadiere*. Manlio, that's me, and that's my brother, Teo.'

'Whose land is this?' Sustrico asked him.

'It's . . . well, it ain't no one's really, *brigadiere*. Our reserve starts over there,' he said, pointing to a line of trees that were marked with big red crosses. 'This bit here . . . well, it's abandoned, like.'

'So,' Sustrico said, 'what were you doing on it?'

Manlio Pastore looked at his brother, sniffed, then wiped his nose with the back of his hand. 'We was following the dog.'

Sustrico stared hard at him. 'Following the dog? What's that supposed to mean?'

'The dog came charging into this patch here, and we came charging after.'

'In the middle of the night?' Sustrico challenged him.

'We start work an hour before dawn, *brigadiere*. That's the law, and the hound's nose is sharpest then. The later you leave it, the trickier it gets. The smell of smoke and people cooking breakfast starts drifting up from the valley – it ruins everything.'

Manlio Pastore dropped down on one knee and ran his hand along the lean flank of the dachshund. 'She's a good 'un,' he said. 'We'd already picked half a dozen *scorzoni* when we heard the shot.'

'*Tuber melanosporum Vitt,*' his brother added, in case they didn't know what a *scorzone* was. 'Black truffle, the winter and spring variety.'

'You heard a shot, and so you came to look . . .?' Sustrico let the question hang.

Manlio Pastore stood up. 'Not right away,' he said. 'Someone shooting guns off in the dark? Too much of a risk, ain't it? Me an' Teo hung back, kept out of sight. It was the dog that did it. We gave them half an hour, or more. As soon as we let her off the leash, she ran up here.'

The only witnesses in the area hadn't seen a thing. Or so they claimed.

'She smelled the blood,' said Teo. 'Got a good nose on her, she has.'

'When we saw the body, I called one-one-three on my mobile.'

'It was five fifty-three when you spoke with me,' said Sustrico. 'Then you waited here until the squad car arrived. Did you hear anyone, or see anything?'

Manlio Pastore shrugged his broad shoulders. 'Like what, *brigadiere*? I told you, didn't I? We heard the gunshot, but we didn't come running. Another *cavatore* got his throat slit out Preci way a few years back. Someone was stealing truffles on his patch, his wife said at the inquest. Whoever the fucker was, they . . . well, *you* lot never caught him, did you?'

He looked steadily from Sustrico to Cangio, from *carabiniere* to park ranger, then back again, as if they were responsible for the murder of a truffle hunter and the failure to catch the person who had killed him.

Cangio looked towards the body, and felt his stomach heave again.

The light was brighter now, the headless corpse even more obscene than it had seemed before. The body had settled back against a big oak tree. The trunk was splattered with blood; fragments of white bone were sticking out of the bark.

'Might he have stumbled on someone poaching on your reserve?' Sustrico asked, nodding over towards the corpse.

The two men exchanged a look.

'Looks like it, don't it?' Manlio Pastore said.

'One thing, though,' his brother, Teo, added. 'There ain't a single hole—'

'What's that supposed to mean?' Sustrico cut in.

'If they was stealing truffles, they didn't find one. Then again, the ranger might have copped them before they started—'

'Pulenti!' Sustrico called sharply to one of his juniors, showing everyone who was in charge. 'Take their names, addresses, phone numbers. That's all we can do until the RCS get here.'

'The what?' Manlio Pastore asked him.

'The Regional Crime Squad,' Sustrico said, and turned to the other *carabiniere*. 'Carosio, go back up to the road and stand beside the patrol car. We don't want them getting lost in the woods, do we?'

Carosio looked at his wristwatch. 'They'll be stuck in the rush-hour traffic coming out of Perugia, *brigadiere*.'

'Just do as you're told,' Sustrico ordered him. 'The sooner they get here the sooner we can get back to work.'

Special constable Pulenti talked with the Pastore brothers, taking notes, while Cangio waited with Sustrico, fighting hard to control his anger.

'Why didn't you tell me straight away that he was dead?'

Sustrico ignored the question. 'When did you last see him?' he asked.

'Yesterday at lunchtime.'

'And?'

'And what?'

'How did he seem?'

'The same as always,' Cangio said.

'Would you care to explain that?'

Two more *carabinieri* came bursting out from the bushes.

'Here comes trouble,' Sustrico muttered as he approached them.

The newcomers were immaculately turned out, wearing peaked caps encrusted with gold braid and silver laurels. Cangio had been expecting senior officers. What he hadn't expected was that one of them would be female.

Women were rare specimens in the armed military police force. Senior female officers were the rarest breed of all. From beneath her cap, a few stiff black curls escaped the bun at the nape of the woman's neck.

The man by contrast was short and skinny, as if he had enlisted in the hope that a uniform might add some lustre to his appearance.

Cangio watched as Sustrico nodded towards the Pastore brothers, then glanced in his direction, speaking all the while to the two senior officers. They were both far younger than Sustrico, not much older than himself. Would the brigadiere tell them what he was doing there, Cangio wondered. After all, he wasn't a witness or a relative of the dead man.

He was the one whose body should have been slumped against that tree.

The woman broke away, leaving her colleague with Sustrico.

'So, you're the partner of the victim,' she said, her lipstick a shade too bright. She didn't wait for confirmation. 'You'll need to come down to the station in Spoleto for questioning.' She pursed her lips at him, but not in a smile. 'We will be handling the investigation, under the local magistrate's direction, of course. Does your partner' – she blew out a sigh – 'sorry. *Did* he have a desk, a locker, time sheets, that sort of thing?'

'We keep logbooks.'

'Good,' she snapped. 'Bring those with you. Yours, too. Files, phonebooks, diary, anything he may have left at work. We'll expect to see you in' – she turned her wrist and stabbed a glance at her watch, 'two hours, max. We shouldn't be here very long once the magistrate, pathologist and forensics team arrive. Please don't keep us waiting. Understood?'

She stared at him for some moments.

'I know who you are,' she said. 'Sebastiano Cangio, right? The park ranger who unmasked a corrupt general of the *carabinieri* and beat a fearsome mafia clan singlehanded.' She pushed a straggling curl back under her cap. 'Do you know who blasted your partner?'

Not *killed*, or *murdered*. *Blasted*.

Was she as tough as she was trying to sound?

'The same people who tried to kill me,' he said. 'The 'Ndrangheta.'

She had a tough smile, too, and she turned it on him.

'That's one hell of a word. 'Ndrangheta. The newspapers love the sound of it, but I doubt they'll be using it on this occasion. The 'Ndrangheta?' She paused, challenging him. 'They'll be keeping a low profile after their unlucky run-in with you, Ranger Cangio.' She touched the peak of her cap. 'I'll see you in town. If you're late, you'll be hearing squad car sirens.'

Sustrico had mentioned trouble coming when the RCS had arrived.

Most of it seemed to be heading for *him*.

TEN

Simone Candelora was driving.

He glanced in the rear-view mirror and lifted his foot off the accelerator. 'Shit! Another one! And you're chucking fag ends out of the car. Do we want to go to jail for starting a forest fire? Use the frigging ashtray!'

The *carabinieri* squad car was too close for comfort, hugging the back bumper as they cruised around a blind bend, but the driver didn't seem to be interested in them. He was looking for an opportunity to overtake.

'That's the second one in three minutes,' Simone said, as the car went whizzing past, accelerating hard. 'Two of them in uniform, the one in the back seat wearing a suit or something. What do you reckon? Magistrate? Doctor?'

'Who cares,' Ettore said, as the squad car disappeared up the road.

Simone glanced at him. There was just no handling Ettore, no telling him. 'You ought to start fucking caring, Ettò! The cops'll be swarming all over the—'

'What was I supposed to fucking do?' Ettore shot back at him.

There was no arguing with him, either.

'Just watch those bloody fag ends. We need to be at the airport and get this business sorted out. Production's up and running, now for the transportation.'

Ettore lit another cigarette. 'You reckon choosing Marra was a good idea?'

Simone Candelora breathed in loudly through his nose. 'We're married to him, Ettò. Divorce is out of the question now. We need the sucker.'

'There's something about him, don't know what it is exactly. He's nervy, know what I mean? Got no fucking backbone. I wouldn't want him speaking to the *carabinieri* while we're away.'

'Why would they waste time on him?' Simone said. 'They've got bigger things to think about this morning. Fuck me!' he said, as another squad car went flying by. 'We just move over and give them room.'

'Fucking rubbish, those Alfas they use. Sloppy suspension.'

'The driver even saluted. Did you see that?'

'They've got a lousy day in front of them,' Ettore said.

At the Treponti turn-off, they headed left for Foligno and the regional airport outside Assisi.

No one offered him a lift.

He was going to have to walk back to where he'd left the Fiat 500.

It was a couple of kilometres to the Vallo di Nera turn-off. Still cold, still dark, tall trees and dense woods pressing in on one side, the sheer cliff blocking out the sun on the other side where the road had been hacked out of the rock. Then something flashed in the darkness among the trees.

He stopped dead, waiting to see if it would flash again.

When nothing happened, he ducked his head and peered through the trees.

The light blinked on again for an instant.

A narrow track led into the forest, tyre treads clearly visible in the damp ground. Though overgrown, it seemed to have been used often enough.

He listened for a moment, then he stepped onto the path and ventured into the woods. Trees hung overhead, blocking out the light. Bushes pressed in closely on both sides, swishing as they caught on his clothes. There were scuffs and footprints in the damp mould, some leading in, others coming out. He hadn't taken more than twenty paces before he pulled aside a leafy branch, and there was the rear end of Marzio's Land Rover.

Had sunlight flashed off one of the wing mirrors?

The Land Rover had obviously been hidden, but not that well. Of course, it all depended on why you were hiding it, and more to the point, who had hidden it: Marzio, or whoever had killed him?

The *carabinieri* hadn't spotted the vehicle, which wasn't surprising. Sustrico and his men were out of their depth in the forest. He wondered whether he ought to tramp back through the woods and tell them about it.

Before he did anything, he decided to check the interior, the glovebox in particular.

He stretched out his hand to open the door, then stopped himself from touching it.

There might be fingerprints.

That's what the *carabinieri* would be looking for.

Then again, the Land Rover was full of fingerprints, his and Marzio's. He slipped his hand inside his sleeve, reached in through the open window, prised up the interior door handle and swung the door open.

The vehicle was ancient, rusty; the door let out a tired groan.

The car keys were missing from the ignition.

Had Marzio taken them with him?

Still covering his hand with his sleeve, he pressed the glovebox button and wrenched it open. Marzio had kept an old Beretta M9 in there. Cangio was still unlicensed, a probationer for another year yet, but Marzio was entitled to carry a pistol and use it in performance of his duties. Given the sort of work they did, it seemed faintly ludicrous, and they had sometimes joked about it.

Would you pull a gun on a tourist or a grey squirrel?

But Marzio never went out on patrol without his pistol.

Apart from an empty Coca-Cola can, the glovebox was empty.

Had they killed Marzio, then taken the gun away from him?

He walked back along the path to the road. He was filled with anger and resentment.

They had shot the wrong man.

'The 'Ndrangheta, you mean?' he imagined Captain Grossi saying.

He couldn't face the idea of confronting her again just yet. He pulled his mobile phone from his pocket, intending to call Sustrico and tell him where to find the Land Rover. While he searched for Sustrico's number, he heard a noise in the air above him. Then he spotted the big, black helicopter, coming closer, circling overhead.

Captain Grossi might be a pain, but she was evidently good at her job.

He phoned Sustrico anyway, told him about the vehicle.

'There should be a service pistol in the glovebox,' he said, before he ended the call.

They'd soon find out that there wasn't.

'*Signor* Marra! *Signor* Marra!'

Rosanna's eyes were wide with fright, her fist pressed to her mouth, as if to stop herself from crying.

'*Signor* Marra, have you heard the news? They've killed a ranger!'

He wasn't sure what his secretary had said. A ranger, a stranger?

He wasn't sure how he had responded, either. Yes, he'd heard, or no, he hadn't.

He rushed into his office, closed the door, and reached for the cigarettes he kept in a drawer for visiting customers. He fumbled with the packet, fumbled with the lighter, managed to get one lit at last, took a puff, and started to cough.

'Fucking hell!'

He went to the window, opened it for a bit of air.

He heard the *put-put-put* coming from the Perugia end of the valley this time, and he stood there watching, waiting until he saw what was making the noise.

A tiny black dot in the sky, growing bigger every second.

It travelled straight for a while, coming right at him, then suddenly it swerved away in a wide circle right over his head, sweeping out over the woods and the reserve, hovering for a bit at one point, then making another sweep, and then another sweep after that one.

'Jesus Christ!'

It was like the last time, six months before. There'd been helicopters circling over the mountains and forests for days when that park ranger had been shot, and a *carabiniere* who'd been double-dealing with the 'Ndrangheta had been arrested. He'd spent most of the time holed up in the office, listening to the racket overhead, praying for all he was worth that the cops would give it up and go home fast.

It was the truffle reserve he was worried about, the land around it . . .

He started mouthing silent prayers again.

They had these gadgets now, infrared, or ultra-something, X-ray cameras, lasers, and that. They could spot all sorts of things from the air. Anything that was hotter or colder than it ought to be showed up in brilliant colour. They could tell where the grass had been recently cut, or the earth had been moved.

The helicopter made another couple of circuits, then headed north again.

He felt giddy, couldn't stand up. Thank God, Simone and Ettore had things to attend to that morning. He wouldn't have wanted his partners to see him in this state.

He sat down at his desk and tried to light another cigarette.

His hands were shaking with fright.

ELEVEN

Ranger Station, Mount Coscerno.

Cangio filled a cardboard box with the clutter from Marzio's desk.

Then he turned to the metal filing cabinet.

It looked more like an improvised kitchen than a piece of office equipment, the top littered with stuff for making coffee: a blue Gaz camp stove, a smoke-stained aluminium Moka, jars of coffee and sugar, a tin of powdered milk, some cups and spoons, and a packet of biscuits.

The filing cabinet consisted of four sliding drawers: one for filed reports and orders, a drawer for him and one for Marzio. Marzio's drawer contained a clean, folded shirt, a change of socks and nothing else; the drawer at the bottom was the only one that could be locked. It was where Marzio kept the service pistol when he wasn't on duty. Marzio kept the key, too. It was probably in one of the pockets of his uniform.

Cangio thought it over for a moment.

Breaking and entering wasn't his forte, but he had to open that drawer. The Beretta pistol might be safely tucked away in the drawer, not stolen from the glovebox of the Land Rover, as he had presumed.

He took a metal paper clip from his own drawer, straightened it out, then formed a hook at one end. He got down on his knees and did some jiggling. The lock turned a bit, but still the drawer wouldn't open. He tried again, then gave the drawer a sudden jab with the heel of his hand. The drawer slid out a bit on its rollers. Not all the way, but far enough for him to reach inside and feel around. The only thing that he found inside the drawer was a pale green file.

There was no sign of the pistol.

Whatever Marzio had been doing in the woods, he had gone out armed and ready for trouble.

The file was government-issue, the sort they used for storing tourist information, statistics regarding wildlife, landslides, poaching, forest fires, and all the other things that could, and did, often happen in the woods and mountains, which put the public at risk.

Why hadn't Marzio kept it in the top drawer with the rest of the files?

Cangio turned it over, read what was written on the cover, and then had to read it again to be sure that he had read it correctly.

Beneath the printed title, *Ministero delle Politiche Agricole e*

Forestali – Corpo Forestale dello Stato, Marzio had added a note in large block capital letters.

STRANGE SIGHTINGS IN THE PARK.

The file was discoloured, as if corroded by contact with the metal cabinet. He felt grains of dust beneath his fingertips as he opened it, and wondered how long it had been lying there. There wasn't much inside the file, just seven sheets of paper, two typed, the others written out in Marzio's bold, distinctive hand.

The first page was dated 02/06/2012, which made it more than two years old.

A doctor with a troublesome prostate had been called out the night before by a patient who lived near Vallo di Nera. Along the way, the doctor had stopped the car to relieve himself. While urinating at the roadside, he had heard strange voices in the woods, speaking a language he had never heard before, then high-pitched squeals of laughter. 'Dim lights were dancing through the trees,' the doctor stated. His patient had told him later that other people living in the area had heard those sounds and seen those glimmering lights.

The general opinion in Vallo di Nera was that the creatures were elves.

Elves?

As if witches and black magic weren't enough!

Weren't elves supposed to live in England or Germany? Had they come over on holiday to sample the woods in Italy? The only elves that Cangio had ever seen were creatures dreamt up in Hollywood. Was that what happened? People went to see a fantasy film, and next thing they were seeing elves all over the place?

At the bottom of the page, Marzio had noted that the doctor was a respected professional, a teetotaller who drank only mineral water on account of his delicate constitution, but he could offer no rational explanation for what the doctor might really have seen.

There was a bit more detail in the next account that Marzio had recorded.

A week or so later, a middle-aged tourist had crashed her car one night on the road outside Vallo di Nera, and died not long after in the hospital in Spoleto following a massive heart attack.

Three tiny, curved figures had darted across the road in front of her, she managed to say. She had lost control of the car while trying not to hit them. Before she died, she had told her daughter that they looked like gnomes or goblins.

'The first goblins ever sighted in Umbria,' Marzio had written neatly at the foot of the page, though there was no indication whether he had taken the report seriously.

Elves and goblins?

He filled the Moka with water, spooned coffee into the filter, then lit the Gaz burner. While waiting for the coffee to percolate, he started on the biscuits as he began reading the next file. He hadn't had time for breakfast after Sustrico phoned that morning.

He finished off the packet, and hoped it would help him get through the rest of a day that promised to be troublesome. What had the female *carabiniere* captain said – something about seeing his face in the local newspapers? As if he was seeking attention. If that wasn't trouble, he didn't know what was. Those two weren't going to listen if he tried to tell them what he thought had really happened, Lucia Grossi had already made that clear.

And if they saw that file of Marzio's . . .

'Elves don't blow people's heads off with shotguns,' he said out loud.

He topped up his coffee cup, read the next case, and the one after that.

They were all pretty much of a muchness, all recorded in the vicinity of Vallo di Nera, and all within the space of a month or so, more than two years earlier.

Two poachers netting birds had heard 'strange noises' in the forest. A band of men hunting wild boar had let off shots when something moved in the bushes, then taken fright when a tiny man jumped out and screamed at them for firing on him, shouting words that might have been curses, though the hunters hadn't understood a thing he had said. Then two more 'little men' had run out of the bushes and dragged the angry one away, the hunters added.

He turned to the last sheet of paper.

An old man riding a bicycle at night had been drawn off the road by three lights flashing on and off in the woods. Will-o'-the-wisps, he had called them. And when he had fallen off his bike, instead of a helping hand, he had received a smart slap on the cheek from Jack-o'-Lantern himself. There had been wild laughter as he abandoned his bike and made his escape.

What had Marzio made of it?

It all seemed so ridiculous. Cangio couldn't believe that Marzio would take it seriously, and yet for more than a month he seemed to have done so. Then, at some point, the reports had stopped. Had he started collecting local tales and legends, only to tire of the subject, put the material away in a drawer and forget all about it? Cangio managed a smile. Had Marzio locked the file away for fear of looking like a fool?

And yet . . .

There was *something* in the tales, however, apart from the mystery of what was described, that made them seem credible. The recurring theme for starters. Three elves, three lights, three curved figures. Each witness reported the same thing, or at least something similar. And there was Vallo di Nera, too. The small town had been mentioned in at least four of the reports. But then, suddenly, the reports had stopped on 09/07/2012. There'd been no more sightings in two years, none that Marzio had bothered to make a note of, anyway.

He put the file back in the bottom drawer and closed it.

If Lucia Grossi thought the 'Ndrangheta was a fairy tale, what would she make of Marzio's hobgoblins?

He picked up Marzio's effects and headed for town.

Cangio looked around the office.

It had changed a lot since the last time he'd been there.

A crucifix was hanging on the wall behind Sustrico's chair, along with a large framed photo of the new pope. Between the phone and the computer stood a plastic bottle in the form of the Virgin Mary wearing a blue plastic crown. *Holy Water from Lourdes*, the label said. Next to the bottle was a bronze bust of Padre Pio, a plaster figurine of the Sacred Heart on the other side.

Was Sustrico warding off evil spirits these days?

He had never considered it from the *brigadiere*'s point of view. Sustrico's life had been turned upside down by what had happened six months before. How did a *carabinieri brigadiere* address a once-mighty *carabinieri* general who was under arrest for corruption and disgracing the uniform that they both wore?

Lucia Grossi was sitting behind Sustrico's desk, a slimline laptop in front of her, typing up Cangio's statement as he made it. Captain Geremia 'Jerry' Esposito sat beside her on a wooden chair, checking his partner's spelling. Sustrico had evidently handed over his office and made himself scarce. Cangio imagined the brigadiere, sitting somewhere with a mug of coffee and a smoke, glad to leave a difficult investigation to the two young, fast-track RCS officers.

They'd been going through the material that Cangio had brought down from the ranger station. It didn't amount to much. There was Marzio's logbook, his address book, a time sheet which recorded when he had been on duty over the last month, framed photos of his wife and their two grown-up daughters, plus a larger one of little Matteo when he was just a few days old. Matteo was Marzio's only grandchild. *At least*, thought Cangio, *the only one that Marzio was ever going to see.*

That thought had stuck in his throat as he was carrying the box out to his car.

The service Land Rover had been found and impounded. They were dusting it down for fingerprints, taking DNA swabs, Jerry Esposito told him, so Cangio would be obliged to use his own transport for the next few days.

'Did you find the Beretta?' he asked. 'He always keeps it in the glovebox.'

No gun had been found in the Land Rover.

'Model?'

'It's an old M9.'

'So,' Esposito concluded, 'the killer's got a pistol now, as well.'

Cangio didn't say a word about the file he had chosen not to bring along.

He didn't want to make a laughing stock of Marzio, or set the *carabinieri* on a time-consuming investigation that would take them nowhere. The file was old, probably irrelevant.

An 'Ndrangheta killer had nothing in common with the characters in fairy tales.

Even these two were bound to see it eventually.

'How come you do all the late shifts?' Lucia Grossi asked him, flicking through the pages of Marzio's logbook.

'Marzio was a family man. I'm a nightbird.'

Jerry Esposito pounced. 'What's *that* supposed to mean?'

'I like being out at night.' Cangio said. 'I spend the late shift watching wolves.'

'Watching *wolves*?' Esposito echoed.

'I'm working on a pamphlet, describing the wolf population in the national park. For visitors, you know?'

'There's nothing here for the last three days,' Lucia Grossi said, holding up Marzio's logbook as if it were a prize piece of evidence at a trial.

'We tend to write a summary report at the end of each week. My log's in the same state. As a rule, I write it up on a Sunday—'

'It sounds most sloppy,' Jerry Esposito cut in.

'Until this happened,' Cangio told him, 'the only recent drama we've had was me being shot by a member of the 'Ndrangheta—'

'That's history,' Lucia Grossi reminded him sharply. 'It's this week we're interested in. What has Marzio Diamante been doing *this* week?'

'I've no idea,' Cangio admitted. It sounded evasive, even to his own ears. 'Still, two rangers, one shot, one dead . . .'

'How would you describe your professional relationship with the deceased,' Lucia Grossi asked him, sounding like a prosecutor in a courtroom.

'We were friends, colleagues . . .'

'Friends and colleagues sometimes argue.'

'Marzio never argued with anyone in his life,' Cangio said emphatically, though he had no way of knowing whether what he said was true. He hadn't known Marzio Diamante eight months before, and Marzio wasn't exactly an open book.

'So what was he doing on his own in the woods?'

At night, and carrying a pistol, Cangio added mentally.

'Wasn't there a note on his desk?' she continued. 'A phone number where he could be contacted?'

'His mobile phone wasn't in the office.'

'It wasn't found on the body, either. Would he go into the woods without his phone?'

'I doubt it,' Cangio admitted.

'If there *was* an emergency, he'd have called you, surely?'

There was a hint of suspicion in the way she tagged on 'surely?' And yet, it renewed the doubts in his own mind, too. Why hadn't Marzio called to tell him what was going on? Had it been something private? Something personal?

'There was no emergency,' Cangio insisted. 'He would have let me know.'

'What other reason could there be, Cangio? You have an idea, I bet.'

'I can't help you on that point,' he said.

Lucia Grossi held his gaze for some moments, then dropped her eyes to the keyboard and started typing again.

Esposito pointed something out on the screen. 'A comma's missing,' he said. Then he turned to Cangio. 'Let's get this straight. Marzio Diamante was doing something you didn't know about. Did he often act on his own initiative?'

Cangio shook his head. 'Not really.'

What would they say if he told them he'd been watched by the 'Ndrangheta, and that Marzio had probably walked into a trap that was intended for him?

'As I said before, Marzio avoided the night shift. He wasn't keen to go out on his own after dark.'

'And what do you make of that?'

'Something unusual happened that made him behave in an unusual way.'

'Stop being evasive,' Lucia Grossi snapped.

'Someone got it wrong last night,' Cangio said.

'*Who* got *what* wrong?'

'If Marzio took a call that was meant for me, and went to check . . .'

'Without telling you,' Esposito added on, while Grossi wrote it all down.

Cangio nodded. 'They killed him by mistake. That's my take on it.'

'*They?*' Jerry Esposito frowned.

'The 'Ndrangheta.'

'He told me the same thing this morning,' Lucia Grossi said quietly, as if she and Jerry Esposito were alone in the room. 'He seems to think his partner caught what was coming his way. They saw a uniform, and . . .'

Esposito let out a shrill whistle, his mouth twisted in a sarcastic grin. 'Seb Cangio vs. the Rest of the World, eh? Ten minutes of fame, then the spotlights go out.' He sat back, stretched his arms, let out a sigh. 'I could understand some hot-headed *carabiniere* taking a shot . . .'

For a moment he was tempted to damn the consequences and walk out of there. Instead, he said. 'That's a grave accusation you're making, Captain Esposito. Would anyone in the *carabinieri* want me dead?'

'General Corsini, perhaps? I don't imagine he's too pleased—'

Lucia Grossi intervened. 'OK, cool it,' she said. 'Let's take a look at your theory, Cangio. Why would the 'Ndrangheta want to eliminate you?'

Cangio was silent for some moments. 'They were moving into Umbria. The region was being rebuilt after an earthquake, as you know. There was big money involved, and they wanted to cash in on the emergency. Umbria's off the beaten track, the local police know nothing about large-scale organised crime. They must have thought it would be easy . . .'

'But you came along, and stopped them.'

Jerry Esposito couldn't help sneering. Maybe it was second nature, Cangio thought.

'They lost a few soldiers, but they haven't abandoned the battlefield.'

'And you think they'd risk it all again for your scalp?'

'I was caught in the crossfire when General Corsini and the 'Ndrangheta started shooting. I'd guessed what was going on. I saw the signs . . .'

'And now you're seeing the same signals?'

'You saw them yourself this morning. Marzio's head was blown off with a shotgun,' he reminded them.

'And you conclude that the 'Ndrangheta killed him, thinking he was you?' Lucia Grossi bit her lip. 'It doesn't say much for their intelligence, does it? I mean to say, the most formidable criminal organisation in Italy wipes out the wrong man?'

'They don't care if an innocent bystander walks into the line of fire.'

'Let me propose a different scenario,' the woman said, pushing a stray curl off her forehead. She rested her elbow on the desk and cupped her chin in her hand. 'Your partner went out last night because he had something . . . particular in mind,' she said. 'He couldn't register it in his logbook, leave a note, or tell anyone where he was going, without getting himself into trouble. But something went wrong. Perhaps he saw something that he wasn't supposed to see, and then . . .' She formed her hand into the shape of a pistol, pointed it at him. '*Boom!*' she said, closing one eye and pulling an imaginary trigger.

Cangio stared back at her, wondering whether it happened to everyone who wore a uniform and carried a gun. Where did their sensibility go? The woman had seen the headless body of Marzio that very morning, yet here she was acting out the part of whoever had killed him.

'That's quite a reconstruction, Captain Grossi,' he said. 'Leaving aside my own theory of the 'Ndrangheta infiltration in the park, what do you think Marzio saw that he wasn't supposed to see?'

She pursed her lips, then smiled at him. 'Given that the victim was wearing his uniform and carrying a gun inside the boundaries of the national park, it might seem likely that he caught someone breaking the park rules. The witnesses who found the body mentioned poaching, but it might be something altogether different. Something less than . . . how can I put it?'

While she was searching for the right word, Cangio thought again of the file he had left at the ranger station. What would these two have made of it?

'Was he concerned . . . obsessed about anything?' Jerry Esposito asked.

'Devil worshippers, desecrated churches, whether Spoleto would win their next match.'

Lucia Grossi's mouth closed, the missing word for ever lost, while Jerry Esposito applauded slowly. 'You see?' he said. 'All you had to do was think for a bit. Would you care to expand on what you've just said?'

Cangio told them about San Pancrazio, the abandoned church in Poggiodomo. Satanism seemed to interest them more than organised crime, and all he wanted to do was get out of there.

TWELVE

The hardest part was still to come.

He was going to have to speak with Marzio's wife.

Brigadiere Sustrico had been sent to Castel San Felice to break the news, Lucia Grossi had told him as he was leaving the *carabinieri* station in Spoleto. God knows what Sustrico had told Linda Diamante. If he was any judge of character, Cangio guessed that Sustrico would have been in and out of the house in five minutes flat, even though Marzio's wife might be able to tell them something vital which would help the investigation.

Loredana would have known how to handle the situation.

She and Linda had been born in Valnerina, and they'd always got on well. But Lori was an hour's drive away in Todi. He had phoned her, of course, told her the bad news, listened to her cry into the phone.

'Do you want me to come home?' she had said through her tears.

He couldn't tell her how much he wanted her to come back. Then again, if there was trouble in store, it was best if she was kept out of harm's way.

'I'll be all right,' he had said. 'I'll let you know about the funeral, OK?'

He drove out of Spoleto, took the Sant' Anatolia tunnel, then turned into Valnerina and headed north.

He knew Linda Diamante, of course, though not so well. He and Lori had made up a foursome with Marzio and his wife on a couple of occasions – a pizza, followed by a game of pool and a late-night beer at the hunters' bar in Scheggino. The girls made quite a contrast: Lori, slim and stylish, but low-key in a sweater, jeans and cowboy boots, while Linda was dressed up to the nines, even to eat a pizza and watch her husband shoot billiard balls around a beaten-up pool table.

He cruised around the bend and caught sight of Castel San Felice.

Standing high on a spur of rock, it was one of many tiny forts strung out along the valley of the River Nera, a walled guard post looking out over an ancient trade route that ran three hundred kilometres from Rome to Ancona on the Adriatic coast. If you ignored the occasional cars and tractors, you could imagine driving around the next bend and ploughing into a legion of marching Roman soldiers.

He parked outside the town gate, then walked up the hill and into the village.

He had been to Marzio's home before, but would have found it even if he hadn't. There was just one street in Castel San Felice, fifty or sixty people living on either side of it, and the majority of them were related by blood or by marriage.

An old woman in a light blue overall, a black scarf on her head, was hanging out sheets from a balcony. She saw him coming, stopped what she was doing and watched him walk up the narrow street between the tall houses facing one another.

'Come for Marzio, have you?' she said, letting out a sigh.

He looked down at his ranger jacket, which he had slipped on before racing out of the house at dawn. Anyone wearing that uniform would be looking for Marzio, it stood to reason.

'Number twenty-seven. It's up at the end on the left.'

Even before he rang the bell, he heard the sounds inside the house.

Bad new travels far and fast, but just how much of it had Sustrico told them?

A girl in her teens opened the door, her eyes red, her cheeks wet with tears, a tissue crushed in her fist. Cangio had no idea who she was, a niece or a neighbour maybe. 'I work with Marzio,' he said.

The girl stepped back and let him in without a word.

The rest of the family had gathered in the living room. And not just Marzio's immediate family. There were twenty people. Perhaps more. Women sat on every chair and sofa, the men standing in a tight circle by an open door which looked out over the valley and the shimmering River Nera. Most of the men were smoking.

Linda stood up as soon as he entered the room.

'Seb . . .' she murmured before her lower lip began to tremble. They each took three or four steps, then met in a tight hug.

'I'm so sorry,' he said.

Linda sobbed, murmuring words that he didn't catch. He felt her shudder as her held her close. He had expected nothing less, but the reality was worse. At the same time, he knew that he had to say something. She would learn all the horrid details of Marzio's death at the inquest.

This was a time for comforting lies, not disquieting truths.

'It happened fast,' he said. 'Marzio didn't feel a thing.'

It sounded hollow, sham, even as the words dripped off his tongue. And there was no way of knowing. How long had Marzio been staring into the barrel of the shotgun before it took his head off? What terror had he felt as he heard the trigger click? What was the last thing that had flashed through his mind? His wife, his daughters, his baby grandson . . .

Next thing, he was sobbing so hard that it hurt.

'It all seems so . . . so unreal,' Linda said, patting him on the shoulder. He had come to comfort her, but it turned out she was comforting him. 'A policeman was here a while ago. From Spoleto, he said, a *carabiniere*. He . . . he told me what had happened.'

Her hand pulled gently on his arm.

'Come and sit with me,' she said.

Two seats flanked a narrow window, cushion-covered blocks of stone cut into the walls. The woods and mountains stretched away to the north, the River Nera flowing south, a veil of mist hanging low above the rich green meadows.

The view seemed timeless, a sort of earthly paradise. Generations of people had sat where they were sitting, looking out at that view, but now the scene was spoiled for both of them.

Marzio had been murdered in those woods, his head torn off by a shotgun.

'What happened last night?' he asked her.

Linda frowned, then clasped her hands together to stop them shaking. 'Nothing much,' she said. 'He didn't have a lot to say over dinner, but that's not unusual. Marzio likes his food. And then he said he was going out.'

'What time was this?'

'Ten o'clock. No, hang on,' she said, pressing her fingers to her forehead. 'Rita had rung. She rings up every night before she puts Matteo to bed so he can give his grandad a kiss. Half past nine, say. After that, well . . . it's all a blank. I fell asleep in front of the TV, then I went to bed. Didn't he call you, Seb?'

'Why would he have called me?'

'I thought he was going out on patrol,' she said, raising her eyes, looking at him. 'He must have called you, that's what I thought. He trusted you, Seb. And if he was going into the woods at night . . .'

Cangio felt embarrassed. Marzio hadn't trusted him at all, hadn't told him what he was doing, hadn't confided his suspicions, though clearly something *had* been going on in the park and he had paid for it with his life.

'Let me get this straight,' Cangio said. 'No one phoned apart from his daughter, and then he went out without saying where he was going?'

Linda nodded. 'He took his torch from the drawer over there, gave me a kiss, and then he went . . .'

Her voice quavered, and she started sobbing.

'He's . . . he's been out quite a few nights recently.' Linda reached out and took hold of his hand. 'He's not like you, Seb. You and your wolves! You don't know how pleased he was when you turned up. He likes his bed too much for working nights. So when you offered to do the late shift . . .'

She stopped in mid-sentence.

'He did say something odd before he went out, though.'

Linda let go of his hand, and turned towards the room, staring at the chest of drawers. She might have been seeing her husband again. The women were praying together now, saying the rosary in a group. The voices died away, all eyes on Linda, as if they thought she might want to join in. When she didn't move, the voices picked up the prayer again.

'What did he say?'

'Something about "the same old story", something like that.'

'What was he talking about?'

Linda shrugged her shoulders, looked back at him. 'I wish I'd asked him, but I didn't. I was watching the telly, while he was mumbling on to himself.'

Linda looked into his eyes, wringing her hands. Then she managed a thin smile. 'He was afraid of ghosts. Did you know that, Seb? That's why he didn't like the night shift. That's why

I was so convinced he'd gone out with you. If not with you . . .'
She shook her head, looked down at her hands. 'The Valnerina's
full of ghosts and saints, but Marzio . . . Well, I think he believed
those tales. If people talk, he said, there's always a bit of truth
in it somewhere. Another time he said, there's never smoke
without a fire.'

They sat in silence for a minute, then Linda touched his hand
again.

She stared at him, her eyes bright with tears.

'Do you think he had a fancy woman, Seb?'

THIRTEEN

S imone and Ettore were standing by the perimeter fence,
gazing through the mesh.
        They were with a man who wore a Customs & Excise
uniform when he was on duty, but now he was wearing black
jeans and a brown leather bomber jacket.

Simone offered him a cigarette. 'All done and dusted, then?'

The man took the cigarette and nodded thanks before he
lowered his head to meet the lighter. 'I checked your stuff through
the customs shed last night.' He pointed to a yellow Boeing 757
cargo jet that was standing on the tarmac, having landed just a
few minutes before. 'She'll be flying out at eleven o'clock.'

Ettore checked his watch. 'And now it's half past nine.'

'They'll start loading her up soon. Flight times are always
ETAs for freight. It depends how much or how little there is at
each scheduled stop. There's not much going out of Umbria these
days, a lot less coming in. The locals blame the crisis, of course,
but what the fuck have they got to export?'

'They've got our fucking truffles,' Ettore said.

The other man laughed. 'Marra Truffles. Sounds good. How
many deliveries are you planning?'

'One a week for starters,' Simone said, 'then see how it goes
from there.'

'Those planes can carry up to ninety thousand kilos, though

the runway here's too short for that much weight. This one started out in Palermo, stopped off in Naples, then on to Rome Ciampino. After Perugia, they'll be flying on to Dusseldorf, then Nijmegen in Holland. By the time she gets to London, they'll be at least half full. Not that there's a problem with the runways in London.'

'What time will that be?' Simone asked.

'She's scheduled to land at four thirty in the morning. The sleepy hour, we call it. We're all pissed off and dying to go home by that time.'

Simone Candelora stamped his foot on the fag end. 'No problems anticipated, then?'

'None at all,' the man replied, taking a final drag before he flicked his cigarette away. 'The guy in London C&E's been well paid.'

'A waste of money,' Ettore said. 'It's only a trial run.'

They watched a blue forklift truck drive out of the customs shed towards the plane, carrying the first of what was to be a weekly consignment of containers on the Dusseldorf–London run. The container wasn't large, but it wasn't small, either. Just right for two thousand jars of truffle paste stacked in fifty large boxes.

'It looks good,' Simone said, admiring the big white letters on a Ferrari-red background.

MARRA TRUFFLES – the world's finest!

'We should have brought Marra,' Ettore agreed, 'let him know how serious we are.'

When the container was safely aboard, Simone handed the customs man an envelope and they shook hands. As he walked away, Simone turned on Ettore. 'Why'd you tell him it was just a dummy run? We want him on board right from the fucking start. We want him shitting bricks in case anything goes wrong. If it does go bollocks, he'll be the first in the firing line.'

'Nothing can go wrong,' Ettore said.

'Make sure it doesn't,' Simone warned him. 'Don Michele's got a lot riding on this, and don't you forget it. No more false moves, OK? There are too many coppers buzzing around as it is.'

FOURTEEN

Cangio stood alone outside the church.

He wasn't superstitious, but he was from Calabria. They had a saying back home: *First in, next out*. If you were the first to arrive at a funeral, the next one would probably be yours. It was better to be safe than to tempt fate.

Besides, fate had not been treating him kindly.

The newspapers seemed to be taking the rumours of Satanism seriously, while he had spent the last two days trying to track down witnesses who proved almost as hard to find as the elves and goblins they claimed they had seen. One had a Swedish name and a telephone number with a Stockholm prefix. Cangio had tried to contact the man a number of times, but no one had ever picked up the phone.

A hill walker from Turin had said he didn't remember the incident. When Cangio read him back a part of the statement he had made to Marzio, the man denied angrily that he had ever said anything of the sort.

The doctor who had stopped to urinate beside the road had died of prostate cancer.

Cangio had managed to speak with his widow on the phone, but the woman had no idea what he was talking about. Her husband had never mentioned seeing anything out in the woods, she said.

Then he had struck lucky.

One of the poachers who had been setting nets for birds turned out to be the owner of a shop selling fishing gear and bait near the Marmore Falls on the River Nera. Cangio had driven down there to speak with him in person, to ask him to verify what he had seen.

It had been like asking a grown man if he still believed in Father Christmas.

'You know how it is,' the man had said. 'The forest at night. It's deceiving, isn't it? You think you've seen a bear, it turns out to be a bush, and nothing else. We were pretty jumpy. I mean to say, we could have got into trouble. What did we really see? God knows . . . Nothing looks the way it really is at night. It could have been anything. We'd had a few drinks as well. Still,' he had admitted, 'I stand by what I told that ranger Diamante. We did see *something*, and we did hear noises, but what it was . . . well now, that's anyone's guess.'

It wasn't much, but it was something.

The village of Caso lay further down the mountain. From this height the tip of a steeple was the only thing visible. Mount Coscerno reared up massively on the other side of the valley. Cangio and Marzio had been planning to put up fences in the area over the next few days. Wild boar were feasting off the local crops. There'd probably be nothing left to save by the time a replacement ranger turned up.

A car pulled into the pine-lined avenue. A big black Mercedes, bringing two official mourners, Alberto Bruni, the director general of the Sibillines National Park, and Mario Simonetti, the executive park ranger.

Cangio's heart sank down to his boots.

He knew them, and they knew him. They had visited him in the hospital in Spoleto six months before, and now they jumped out of the car, homing in on him like a pair of guided missiles.

Cangio saluted, and the director suggested that they move out of the bright sunshine. From the lee of the church, they watched as a coach arrived and unloaded a platoon of uniformed men that Cangio didn't know.

'They're mostly from Abruzzo,' the executive ranger remarked.

Men that Marzio had never met, Cangio realised. *What was the point?*

'A formal send-off,' the director general said, reading his mind, as he offered a cigarette to the executive ranger, then offered the packet to Cangio, too. Cangio didn't smoke very often, but there was something in the gesture that said they were in the same boat together.

'A woeful business,' the director general said with a sigh.

The executive ranger nodded. 'Let's hope the police get to the bottom of it quickly . . .'

'And with as little fuss as possible,' Bruni added emphatically.

'Whatever the cause, Marzio Diamante was in the wrong place . . .'

'At the wrong time,' Simonetti tagged on.

The director general grunted approval, as if to say *And there's an end to it*.

Cangio blew out smoke and bit his tongue. He felt like smashing their empty heads together. They were building up to something, he could feel it.

'Front-page news,' the director general said.

'The sort of publicity we need to avoid.'

'The minister was on the phone this morning. A murder first, and now the occult!'

'Poachers,' Mario Simonetti hissed. 'We're all agreed on that, I hope. A bit of folklore's fine, but Satanists and Devil-worshippers! The tourists would be terrified. It would be the end of everything we've worked for.'

Cangio recalled their visit to the hospital six months before. First, compliments for having faced up to the 'Ndrangheta single-handed, risking death at the hands of General Corsini. Then Director Bruni had clenched his teeth and said: 'The less we say about this deplorable affair the better it will be for everyone.'

Suddenly, the director general crushed out his cigarette and turned on Cangio.

'Have you been talking to the press *again*?'

Cangio dropped his cigarette. 'I've only spoken with the *carabinieri*,' he said.

'Such rubbish in the newspapers! And now the TV's got hold of it.'

For an instant Cangio was tempted to unbutton his lips and tell them that it looked as though the 'Ndrangheta had moved into the park again, and that there might be more than one ranger dead before things got any better.

Instead, he led them off in another direction. 'Without Marzio,' he said, 'I'll need some help, Director General. A replacement officer.'

'That's for the ministry to decide,' Bruni said, raising his nose, sniffing the air. 'With winter coming on, you won't be busy, will you?' He took a step forward and laid his hand on Cangio's shoulder. 'I mean to say, a young chap like you, full of initiative,

I'm sure you can muddle along, at least until the case is closed. Then, well . . .'

Cangio nodded, translating thus: *My career comes first, young man. As soon as this case is history, I'll see what I can do for both of us.*

'What do the *carabinieri* have to say?' Simonetti asked him.

Cangio, being full of initiative, pointed down the avenue.

'Here they come,' he said. 'You can ask them directly.'

Simonetti looked down his nose, then turned away as a dark blue Alfa 159 skidded to a halt behind Cangio's ancient Fiat 500 and the director general's black Mercedes. Two and a quarter cars, Cangio thought to himself, comparing the size of the vehicles. The driver of the Alfa must have thought the same. Instead of cutting the motor, he accelerated with a spray of pebbles and parked the car in another spot closer to the church.

Brigadiere Sustrico got out of the rear door.

He advanced towards them, cap in hand, head bowed. He shook hands with Bruni and Simonetti, and might have offered his hand to Cangio too, but Bruni took him by the arm and leant close to his ear. 'Any news, *Brigadiere*?'

Sustrico shook his head. 'We'll have to wait for the lab reports, I'm afraid. My instinct tells me that this was just an unlucky meeting. Diamante must have bumped into someone who was up to no good.'

'Poachers,' Alberto Bruni insisted. 'Armed and desperate, it goes without saying.'

Cangio left them to their small talk.

A silver hearse turned into the avenue, followed by a long line of family saloons.

As the hearse pulled up, then reversed towards the church doors, he couldn't help but notice that it dwarfed both the *brigadiere*'s Alfa Romeo and the director's Mercedes. There ought to have been a coffin inside the base-extended Jaguar XJ, but he couldn't see it for the mass of wreaths and flowers that filled the rear compartment. As car doors opened and people got out, hanging back in tight groups, an altar boy in a black cassock and lace-frilled surplice came running to unlock the church doors.

Brave boy, Cangio complimented him silently.

The first one in . . .

A priest in purple robes came next.

Then Linda Diamante made her way towards the church, her friends and family close behind her. Linda looked desolate in an ill-fitting black suit. She hadn't expected to lose Marzio so soon, and the clothes she had evidently borrowed made her look far older than she really was. She crushed a white handkerchief to her mouth, glanced over at Cangio, then looked away quickly, as if she had nothing to say to him.

A hand touched his sleeve, then slid beneath his arm. Lips brushed his cheek.

'Leave it to the *carabinieri* this time, Seb.'

As Loredana's hand slid away, he caught hold of it.

'You made it, then,' he said.

He tried to sound detached, but that was not how he felt. He was glad to see her.

'They've put me on the afternoon shift,' she said. 'I have to be back by three. They weren't happy about it, but I told them I owed it to Linda and to Marzio's family.'

Linda and Marzio's family.

He didn't come into it at all. There'd be no sleeping over tonight.

'You be careful in the woods,' she warned him. 'Don't do anything foolish.'

He let go of her hand as they moved towards the church. A black leather jacket and slim-fit black jeans showed off her figure and made her hair seem even darker than it was. Her eyes were glistening brightly, but not on his account.

'What do you want me to do, run away?'

'I don't want someone phoning me to say there's going to be another funeral. You were lucky the last time,' she said with a heavy sigh as they were sucked into the crowd pressing into the church.

An usher asked them if they were family.

'We're with Linda,' Lori said, and the man directed them to the pews at the front on the left-hand side where Linda Diamante and her family were sitting. The church was packed with local people, then row upon row of park rangers.

The altar boy swung a gold-plated thurible on a long chain and the Mass began.

Cangio stood up, or knelt down, following the lead of people near them who seemed to know what to do. His eyes fell often on the coffin propped on trestles in front of the altar.

Would *his* funeral have been like this? Would his parents have travelled from Calabria to bury him in Umbria, or would they have taken him back home before they buried him?

Would Lori's face have shown the distress that marred the face of Linda?

He wasn't a local man. The church would have been half-empty. Still, among so many people, was it possible that no one knew what Marzio had been doing in the woods that night?

He turned his head. Bruni and Simonetti had tagged themselves onto Linda's family, looking suitably humbled in the wake of the calamity of an awkward death. The park rangers sitting behind them looked bored for the most part.

Then Cangio's gaze fell on a man whose face he recognised.

He whispered in Lori's ear. 'Who's the man at the end of the bench?'

'Antonio Marra,' she murmured. 'He went to school with Marzio.'

Marra's face seemed to express a grief that went beyond what you might expect of an old schoolmate.

'Were they close friends?'

Lori shook her head. 'I don't know,' she said.

'Marzio was found near his reserve,' Cangio said.

The woman next to Marra was kneeling now, hands clasped in prayer, her eyes shut tight. She looked like something out of a cheap horror film. Fifty years old, in black weeds, her hair dyed black but showing grey at the roots, her eyes made up as two spectral rings like one of those masks from a Greek tragedy.

'Who's Morticia Addams?' he whispered.

'Maria Gatti,' Lori said. 'D'you know what she does?'

'Scares crows?'

Loredana made the sign of the cross, while Cangio watched the strange woman dressed in black.

'She's a medium,' Lori whispered.

'She's certainly got the looks for it.'

When the service ended, he walked Loredana to her car. 'Tell Linda I'm sorry,' she said. 'I haven't got time to go with them to the cemetery. Are you going?'

'Sure,' he said, his thoughts drifting elsewhere. Bruni and Simonetti would be at the cemetery, breathing down his neck, warning him not to speak to the press.

'Hey! Are you listening to me?' Lori said. 'Leave it alone, Seb. Don't get involved, OK?'

'OK, OK,' he said, his eyes on Marra and the witch at his side.

Marra was still upset, it seemed, the woman's hand on his shoulder, as if she wanted to help him bear the weight. They were climbing into a newish-looking Porsche that must have cost a fortune.

'I'll call you tonight,' Lori said through the open window.

'OK,' he said again, but the car was already driving away.

FIFTEEN

'**M**YSTERIOUS DEATH IN THE NATIONAL PARK. *'Local people have long been afraid to enter the park at night. Fanatical sects worship the Devil by the light of the moon, sacrificing black cats on the altar stones of abandoned country churches,'* Simone Candelora read the article aloud, his lips pressed close to the phone.

'Alongside the Catholic mysticism for which Umbria is renowned – the saints, Francis of Assisi, Rita of Cascia, and Benedict of Norcia, to name but a few, are revered throughout the Christian world – there is rising undercurrent of Satanism in central Italy, a senior police officer said today—'

He stopped short as Don Michele let out a grunt.

'The cops are chasing weirdos, is that what you're telling me?'

'That's the way it looks,' Simone said. 'We've got nothing to worry about. It might help to frighten off the nosy parkers.'

Was his voice too chirpy, he wondered. Would the don be convinced by it? You needed facts to convince Don Michele.

'We're right on course,' Simone said, adopting a brisk and businesslike tone. 'The plant's up and running now. The product's ready. We've got the local airport sorted, and the dummy load went through OK. The other consignments will be going out next, no problem. I told you, boss, this place is perfect.'

'It *was* perfect,' Don Michele snapped, 'Now the rubberneckers'll be on their toes. They won't all fall for that Devil-worship stuff. A headless body in the woods? That's not what I had in mind.'

'Take it easy, Don Michè,' Simone protested. 'Like I said before, it ain't all bad.'

'What about that other ranger, Cangio?'

That was what was bothering Don Michele.

'What about him? What can he do?'

'You keep Ettore away from him, that's my point.'

'Sure thing,' Simone said, wondering what else he could say to salvage the situation.

There was silence for a bit, then Don Michele said, 'Don't fuck it up, Simò.' Definitive. An order. More than an order. A threat. 'I don't intend to fail in Umbria again.'

Then Simone heard the click of a lighter, the sharp intake of breath.

'These people doing their thing in the woods at night . . .' Don Michele was silent for a bit, taking it in, working it out. 'You know, Simò,' he said at last, 'maybe we can make this Satan business work to our advantage.'

The line went dead.

Simone realised that the phone in his hand was dripping with sweat.

He cut two lines of coke on the bedside table, and snorted hard.

SIXTEEN

'Didn't you get shot, or something?'

The ranger rubbed the back of his neck and seemed embarrassed.

Antonio Marra felt damp beneath the armpits, but he didn't intend to let the ranger know how nervous he felt.

'I saw you on the news.'

Cangio cut him off quickly. 'That isn't why I'm here, *Signor*

Marra,' he said. 'I'm interested in something that may have happened near your truffle reserve more than two years ago, and I was hoping that you might be able to help me.'

Was the ranger playing cat and mouse, or was he bumping around in the dark?

'*May have happened? Two years back?* That's precision for you!'

The ranger held up his hands in a dumb show of surrender.

'It seems to have happened on a number of occasions,' he said with an apologetic smile, running his fingers through his hair. 'And always in the same area. Near your truffle reserve, as I mentioned, *Signor* Marra.'

The more embarrassed the ranger got, the better Antonio Marra felt about it.

'This isn't an official inspection, then?'

'No, it isn't. It's just that we received some reports . . .'

'Two years ago? And you're checking them *now*?'

'I don't know if they were ever followed up.'

'What sort of reports?'

'Strange things going on at night in the woods.'

Marra felt a steel claw grab his guts and give them a twist.

The ranger had been front-page news for a bit. A tenacious twat, though the journalists had used words better suited to a family audience. He'd got himself shot playing silly buggers with a crooked *carabiniere* general. Now, here he was, wondering if anything odd had been going on in the truffle reserve two years before.

Antonio Marra shifted a pile of papers across his desk, his way of saying he had better things to do than waste time talking about the distant past. He felt like telling the kid to go and screw himself, but that was one thing he couldn't do. He would just have to play along and show willing.

'Who remembers what happened last week?' he said, with a wave of his hand.

He regretted it immediately. Marzio Diamante had been murdered, hadn't he? He had to tone down the sarcasm. 'Sorry about that, just joking, officer. Tell me more. If I can do anything to help, I most certainly will.'

Cangio took a seat and told him about the reports his partner had received.

'Poor Marzio,' Marra said. 'Me and him go way back. Not particularly close, of course, but I'd known him since school days. God rest his soul.'

'I saw you at the funeral,' the ranger said.

Marra nodded, tried to contain his surprise. 'Duty, wasn't it? So, what's all this about the woods, then?'

'As I mentioned, a number of people reported strange night-time activity in the vicinity of your truffle reserve. I was wondering whether you might remember hearing or seeing anything out of the ordinary.'

Antonio Marra felt ill, the ranger sitting there, looking at him.

He was going to have to say something.

'These people,' he said, and tapped his temple with his fore-finger. 'The world's full of headcases, right?' He bit his tongue. He had to stop sounding so bloody snotty. 'Do you fancy a coffee, officer?' He picked up the internal phone. 'My secretary—'

'No, thank you,' the ranger said. 'I spoke to one of these witnesses yesterday. He was out in the woods one night with a friend setting nets to catch starlings. It's illegal, as you probably know, so they could have ended up on a charge. Even so, they came forward at the time, saying that they had heard a loud scream. This was in July, the summer before last.'

Marra shrugged his shoulders, his heart racing. 'Animals often screech at night,' he said.

The ranger pulled a file from his shoulder bag. 'Let me read you what they reported.'

Marra watched as he searched through a sheaf of papers.

He had a file . . . a fucking file!

'Here it is: *We were fifty metres away, and the moon was quite bright. We saw two creatures bending over something stretched out on the ground. They were small and wild-looking, making strange jabbering noises.*'

Marra tried to laugh, though it sounded more like a grunt. 'By the light of the moon? Fifty metres away? In the middle of the forest at night?' He clasped his hands together, then rested his elbows on the desk. 'And you're asking me for an opinion?'

He congratulated himself on the tone of his voice. It sounded snappy now, amused, patience stretched, but still trying to help.

The ranger shifted uncomfortably in his seat as if he, too, harboured doubts.

Antonio Marra shook his head. 'Never trust a poacher, officer. Two of them? Giving themselves an alibi, I bet. They'll have dreamt it up. An excuse, you know. Us, officer? *We* weren't doing a thing. I wouldn't set much store by that sort of witness.'

Cangio pulled a face as if to say *That's possible.*

Marra slapped his hands down lightly on the desk like a man playing the bongos.

'I'm sorry, officer, but I've got a busy day ahead of me. Just let me ask you a question before you go. Do you really think these cock-and-bull tales have got anything to do with the death of poor old Marzio?'

A perplexed frown creased Cangio's brow. 'I don't think so,' he said. 'Still, something in these stories evidently attracted his attention. I . . . I just wanted to spread the net a little bit wider.'

'Like those two poachers netting starlings?'

The ranger smiled and stood up. 'Thanks for your time, *Signor* Marra.'

He jumped to his feet. 'No trouble at all. I'll have a word with my employees. You never know, do you? Someone may have heard a bit of gossip. I doubt it, but, well . . . Two years ago, you said?'

'Between June and July. And then, suddenly, it all just stopped. As if the ghosts had disappeared,' he said.

'That's what they do, don't they?'

'What? Sorry?' The ranger had been distracted, putting his file away.

'Disappear. Ghosts, I mean.'

As Cangio left the building, Marra watched him from the window.

His knees were shaking as the ranger drove away. It was all he could do to get back to his desk and collapse in his seat. He pulled out his mobile phone, hands shaking as he searched for the number.

'Maria,' he whispered, the instant she answered, 'I'm in the shit again.'

SEVENTEEN

The breakfast room had the most spectacular view he had ever seen.

OK, he'd been out east, stayed in luxury hotels, seen those pearl-white beaches out on Phi-Phi island, places like that, but they were just exotic, dreamland locations. Within a week you were bored out of your skull. There was nothing doing, no way of getting ahead out there; the king and the military junta of Thailand had the whole place buttoned up.

Here, it was different. Here, you were building an empire, taking back what others had already grabbed. Here, you weren't just some rich boozer on a desert island for a week, leaving paradise to the next bedazzled piss artist the week afterwards. Here, the world was waiting to be taken in hand, waiting to be subdued, waiting to be ruled.

That was how Don Michele saw it, and that was how Simone saw it.

He poured himself more coffee, broke the end off the brioche, popped it into his mouth, then stared out of the window at the elegant line of the Roman bridge and aqueduct with its nine irregular arches, the mass of the medieval castle perched on a rock on this side of the gorge, a smaller fortress at the other end of the bridge where the mountain suddenly reared up towards the sky.

If I ruled the world . . .

The song kept on rattling through his brain.

'More coffee, sir?' a voice murmured at his elbow.

He didn't – couldn't – look away, he just said no.

Looking at that bridge had him seeing zeros. An endless line of them, all the cash you could make, as if each solid stone was a plastic pack of coke weighing twenty kilos. Umbria was a goldmine waiting to be discovered. Put a turnstile at each end of the bridge; charge a euro a shot to walk across and back. Or jump off, if that was what you fancied doing. The locals called it Lovers' Leap, though ninety-nine per cent of the people who jumped were single. An eighty-metre drop to the rocky floor below – death guaranteed. Most people did it every day – walked across, not jumped – stopping at the arched viewing window in the centre, admiring the panorama, pointing to the hotel and the picture window where he was sitting at that very moment.

If I ruled the world . . .

I'd buy this place, he thought.

'Who owns that bridge?' he asked, calling the young waitress over with his finger.

The lass did a double take. 'Owns it?' she said. 'The . . . the town, I think, sir.'

'Who owns this hotel, then?'

Her eyes opened wider. 'The owner's name is *Signor—*'

A telephone rang on a table in the corner, and she jumped. 'Excuse me, sir, I'm alone on duty. I have to answer it.'

'Go ahead,' he said. 'You can tell me later.'

He watched her graceful slalom between the tables, shifting her hips and bum to avoid colliding with the chairs. Buy the hotel, he thought, you'd own the bit of road outside that runs beneath the castle and round to the bridge. That was the place for the first turnstile. Right there, in front of the hotel door. The fortress on the far side of the bridge was a ruin, which probably meant it really did belong to the local council. Just slip a bulky envelope stuffed with big bills to the right man.

The girl came waltzing back. 'There's a gentleman in reception asking for you, *Signor* Candelora. I told them to send him through to the breakfast room. Is that all right, sir? Oh yeah, the name of the owner—'

'Later,' he said, as the visitor walked into the room.

Aldo Capaldi the finance manager was wearing a tracksuit and a pair of Adidas trainers.

'You'd better bring another pot of coffee, too,' he told the girl.

'Certainly, sir.'

Capaldi sat down at the table without waiting to be asked. 'Good morning,' he said.

'You been jogging?'

'Walking around the castle and across the bridge,' Capaldi said, clamming up as the waitress came back. They sat in silence while she poured fresh coffee, only speaking once she'd left them in peace. 'I do it every morning,' he said. 'My constitutional. I thought you ought to know. Antonio Marra was in again yesterday afternoon.'

'Another personal loan?'

Marra had started spending on the basis of the capital the don had put into Marra Truffles. First, the new car, then a planned extension on his house. Like *he* ruled the fucking world.

'Not that,' Capaldi said, breaking in on his thoughts. 'He was talking about repaying the loans and cancelling the mortgage, paying it all back.'

Simone sipped his coffee. 'How would he do that?'

'He's thinking of selling out. Getting rid of the business.'

Alarm bells sounded in Simone's head. 'Who would he sell it to?'

'He mentioned you,' Capaldi said, wiping sweat from his brow with the sleeve of his tracksuit. 'It stands to reason, doesn't it? You've already put so much into the company; the best way to guarantee your investment would be to buy out the other partner. That's the way he sees it. I thought you'd like to know before he tells you. He was asking me to tot up the total value minus debts and repayments. He'll double it or triple it, depending on what he thinks he can get away with, then he'll make you a proposal.'

'We aren't buying,' Simone said.

Capaldi sipped his coffee and sat in silence for some moments.

'There've been some ups and downs at Marra Truffles,' he said at last. 'I mean to say, more downs than ups, though you know all that, of course. You could play him at his own game, buy it cheap, turn it into a respectable earner probably, but, well . . . while Marra's there, you'd never have a good name. He's always getting himself into scrapes of one sort or another.'

'What sort of scrapes?'

Arnaldo Capaldi gulped down his coffee. 'Just rumours, things you hear. Nothing specific, nothing criminal, though. I'll see what I can find out.'

'You do that,' Simone said.

The finance manager glanced at his watch, stood up. 'Just time to go home, have a quick shower, change my clothes, then off to work,' he said.

'Let me know if you hear from him again, OK?'

Simone went out onto the balcony at the hotel rear, lit his first cigarette of the day and stared at the bridge.

So much for the golden boy.

What had Antonio Marra been up to?

If he did have skeletons rattling around in his cupboard, Don Michele wasn't going to like it.

EIGHTEEN

Two-thirty. A cold, clear night, the sky full of stars.

Cangio was up on the mountain again.

He'd been watching the wolves for an hour, or more.

Suddenly, the pack leader circled around them, his teeth bared, snarling, and the younger males dropped down on the ground. The leader was enormous, lean and black haired, far bigger than a German sheep dog.

The wolves had eyes that sparkled like gem-stones in the night-vision glasses.

They'd been hunting for rabbits, surrounding a warren built into a bank, growling down into the tunnels, scaring the rabbits so much that they tried to dash out of the other exits. An organised slaughter. A culling, if that was what you wanted to call it. The younger ones were learning how to kill.

But now the pack was silent and still.

He was up on the boulder outcrop. He could see the woodlands above Vallo di Nera, the truffle reserves at the foot of Mount Bacugno. It was an excellent vantage point. He could keep an eye on everything that moved: the hunters and the hunted. Until that moment only the barking of the wolves and the screams of the rabbits had disturbed the night.

The leader was standing over the others now, his tongue lolling out of the side of his mouth.

Despite his hooded jacket, Cangio was freezing cold, a crisp breeze blowing into his face. Downwind, the wolves couldn't smell him, hadn't been frightened off by his scent though he was less than two hundred metres away.

The wolf's head turned, and a moment later Cangio heard the rumble of gears, a distant roar of rubber on the empty road down below in the valley.

Their sense of hearing was amazing.

The younger wolves raised their ears, sniffed the air, then settled down again, as if they knew that the sound presented no threat.

'Have you heard that noise before?' he asked out loud.

He slid forward on his elbows and knees to the edge of the rocky platform. He could see the road more easily from there. He shifted his night-vision glasses and stared down into the valley. He spotted the antlers of a stag gleaming white in a thicket, but he kept on moving left until he picked out four fluorescent beams of light, two vehicles, the headlights coming and going behind dark, dense clumps of trees that grew between the river and the road.

Suddenly, the lights swerved left, one set after the other, then they went out altogether.

He focused the glasses, but it didn't help. Not at that distance. There was nothing to see, just shadows fragmenting and breaking up, leaving splintered imprints on the lenses like a flickering silent movie.

He glanced at his watch.

Two forty-two.

Had they started working nights at Marra Truffles, he wondered. There was a planning permission notice outside the gates. Marra was building an extension on empty space at the rear of the factory, expanding the business, people said. Were lorries travelling in with building materials by night to avoid the daytime traffic?

He shifted the night-glasses to the woods where Marzio's body had been found just beyond Marra's truffle reserve. Everything was dark over there, no sign of lights or movement. He really would have liked to stop in at the factory on his way home and ask the drivers if they had been working the night that Marzio died – ask them if they'd seen anything.

He moved the glasses over the woods where the road wound up to the summit of Mount Bacugno. That was where the 'elves' had been spotted, if Marzio's reports could be relied on.

Two years before . . .

Antonio Marra had been trying to expand his company then, as well, but the work had come to a sudden halt.

Just like the 'strange sightings.'

'An anonymous complaint,' the clerk at the courthouse in Spoleto had told him when she pulled the file from the archive that afternoon. 'It didn't go to court for lack of evidence. But that put an end to his ambitions.'

An unlucky man?

'No head for business,' the clerk confided.

She was in her late fifties, a daunting woman, with dyed ginger hair and big round tortoiseshell glasses. She gave the impression that she knew a lot, but wouldn't tell you a thing without a warrant signed by a magistrate. And yet, with so much power at hand, why waste it?

'There was talk of some . . . irregularity,' she murmured, resting her chin on her hand.

'Irregularity?'

'Those woods are protected.'

'What was going on?'

The woman stared at him, her grey eyes clouding over.

'No action was taken,' she said, 'but . . . something wasn't *right*.'

She pronounced the word *right*, as if wrong was an unthinkable.

'With the land?'

He had tried, but she wasn't going to tell him any more. He could understand it if she was talking about the truffle factory. There were rules and regulations, health and hygiene, safety, and so on, but the land?

'Something not quite . . . *right*,' she had said again, 'but it was never proved.'

Cangio turned the binoculars back on Marra Truffles.

There were no lights, no sounds now.

Maybe they had an underground garage, or a loading bay.

He turned back to the mountain, looking for the wolves again.

The pack had disappeared while he had been distracted.

Had they gone down to the valley, hunting for hens and sheep?

He cursed himself for having let them out of his sight.

He cursed for having lost sight of the trucks in Marra's compound.

NINETEEN

Two-thirty.

Antonio Marra was standing by the window.

The sky was clear and full of stars, but it was freezing out there.

Then the sound of motors broke the silence, wheels crunching hard on the gravel as two trucks pulled into the compound, ground to a halt, then switched off their headlights and engines.

As the drivers jumped down, Simone and Ettore stepped forward to greet them.

Marra drew back from the window, collapsed in the padded chair behind his father's desk, head in his hands. He had been directing his company from behind that desk ever since the day his dad had passed away.

Thirteen years now, for better or worse.

Worse, he conceded in a flash of deep despair.

It wasn't his company any more, except on paper in the form of bills to pay and phoney contracts to sign. If he'd been running things, he wouldn't be cowering inside his office like a dog some careless owner had forgotten in the car, having more important things to think about. He was doing only what he was told to do, and nothing more than that. Let *them* get their hands dirty. His hands were black enough already. Simone had told him to be there to sign receipts for the incoming merchandise.

He was smoking when Ettore came crashing into the room and dropped two sheets of paper on the desk. The dockets were made out to a company in Reggio Calab—

'Don't read 'em, Antò,' Ettore said. 'Just fucking sign 'em.'

Building materials.

Shit was what they were bringing in.

And he was up to his neck in it.

Antonio Marra signed his name, trying to stop the pen from shaking.

He was sliding deeper into a nasty hole that he had dug for

himself. Simone had offered him a hand to jump into it, and Ettore pushed him back whenever he tried to crawl out of it. They were both evil, each in his own way, that was the truth of it. The trouble was, if they went down, they'd be taking him with them.

'Move it,' Ettore growled, watching as he stamped the sheets with *Marra Truffles International* in blue ink, then wrote *Received* and the date on top of the ink stamp.

With each signature, he felt himself slipping further away.

How the hell was he supposed to get out of it?

Had he signed his own death warrant this time?

'Right,' Ettore said, sweeping up the papers. 'Fuck off home, then.'

Maria Gatti had read the tarot cards, but that was a disaster, too. Maria saw black in every card, predicting danger for him and trouble for the company.

Even death, she had said the last time.

Maria was never wrong when it came to reading the cards.

TWENTY

Cangio knocked on the front door.

The Pastore brothers knew the local woods and the people who frequented them.

Might they have heard about the strange sightings mentioned in Marzio's file?

He had left it late in the day before stopping by, in the hope of finding them at home. It was twenty to six. Too early for dinner. Too early for drinking – not that that would stop anyone with a real thirst. If the brothers weren't home, they could be anywhere, and they might not come back until late.

He knocked again, but harder this time.

The cottage where they lived was in perfect order, he noted, standing back, taking it all in. The stone walls had been freshly pointed, the wooden windows and shutters varnished, a smart coat of green paint on the front door. After the last earthquake, the area around Vallo di Nera had been extensively rebuilt. It looked as if the brothers had claimed the EU funds and set their home in order. Had they done the work themselves, he wondered. A lot of people had. In which case, they'd have a shed or a workshop, a garage, maybe, where they kept their tools.

He decided to have a look around the property.

Two ground-floor windows were barred on the far end of the house, as if they feared thieves. As he turned the corner, he heard faint sounds behind a thicket of bushes. A path of large stones set in the cropped grass led into a grove of bushes.

He hadn't taken three steps when a dog started barking.

'Who goes there?' a voice growled.

Next thing, he was facing a dark shadow with a shovel raised like an axe.

'Ranger bloody Cangio,' came the voice again, the shovel slowly falling as the hand that was holding it relaxed. Manlio Pastore was blocking the pathway, a cigarette dangling from the side of his mouth, the yapping dachshund hiding behind his rubber boots. 'What are you doing here?'

'I was looking for you,' Cangio said. 'I tried the house, but no one answered.'

'We're in the shed,' Pastore said. 'Bottling.'

Without another word he turned away, so Cangio followed him.

It was more of a barn than a shed, with chains and padlocks hanging from the doors.

Teo was working, sitting on a stool by a sink, the tap running continuously. He took what looked like a lump of mud from a basket, held it under the tap, then rubbed it with a stiff brush until a truffle materialised, like a gleaming black miniature model of the human brain.

'The truffle season'll soon be closing,' Manlio said. 'We're putting some big ones aside for Christmas. Prices go soaring up then, see. They keep well in the freezer.'

As he cleaned each truffle, Teo dropped it into a plastic bag.

He nodded at Cangio, though he didn't say a word.

'I was wondering whether you might be able to help me,' Cangio said.

Manlio dropped his cigarette, and ground it out. 'How's that, then?'

Cangio took a moment to gather his thoughts.

'Marzio Diamante was working on something – an investigation, let's call it. I don't exactly know what it was about, because he didn't tell me. But he left some notes behind which mention strange goings-on in the woods at night two years ago. Have you any idea what he might have been thinking of?'

Manlio glanced at his brother. 'Well, there's strange, and there's *strange*, ain't that right, Teo?' He turned back to Cangio. 'You can find just about anything in the woods, if you look long and hard enough for it. There's four-leafed clover, three-legged boars, two-legged thieves – them's the poachers. What sort of "strange" was you thinking of?'

'Marzio spoke to a number of people who'd reported seeing' – he felt almost embarrassed as he put it into words – 'elves and goblins . . . fairies, let's say, wandering around in the dark and making a noise.'

'There's loads of fairies,' Manlio said with a grin. 'Quite a few whores n'all. But elves . . . that's a tough one, that is.' He turned to his brother. 'Leave up on them for a bit, will ya! That bag's about full to busting. You ever seen an elf, Teo? In the woods, like, when the lights go out?'

Teo shook his head. 'Not me,' he said. 'I'd run a mile.'

Cangio smiled, but only for a moment.

Was that the point? Was that what those stories had been aiming at: making people run a mile in fright to keep them away from something they weren't supposed to see? You wouldn't tell anyone – most people wouldn't – in case your wife or husband thought you were bonkers. The few people who had spoken to Marzio had been brave souls, indeed.

'So, what does go on in the woods at night?' Cangio insisted.

'Your mate got murdered for a start,' Manlio said. 'We lock our doors, I'll tell you that. The dog sleeps in the kitchen, safe behind bars. Worth a fortune, she is. We've lost . . . what is it, Teo, three dogs, in the last twenty years?'

Teo nodded. 'The last one was pupping, remember?'

Manlio dropped down on one knee beside the dachshund, looking up at Cangio. 'You know what a decent truffle hound's worth? We wouldn't sell her for . . . well, for nothing. We've turned down two thousand euro for a dog, we have. A bitch that's carrying's worth three times as much. The bastards steal them here, drive them up to France, then sell them there. Nasty things go on after dark around here, I can tell you. They'll nick your dogs, your truffles, your tools, your car . . .' He pointed at Teo and laughed. 'They'd nick him, too, if he weren't so friggin' ugly!'

'All this goes on in your truffle reserve?'

'Not all the time, and not just on ours, but it happens.'

'And that's where Marzio's body was found.'

'No, no,' Manlio corrected him. 'He wasn't found on *our* reserve. That bit of woods belongs to no one. It's old common land, that. It's nearer Marra's reserve than it is to ours. Your mate was killed near Antonio Marra's land. We only went in there because the dog ran off, and we chased after her.'

'I know you've spoken to the *carabinieri*.'

'Right bloody useful *they* are!' Manlio snorted. 'They seem to think we killed him!'

'So, what do you think he was doing there?'

'You were his partner,' Manlio said. 'What can *you* come up with?'

'I wouldn't even begin to guess.'

Manlio Pastore rubbed his chin. 'Whatever it was, he got his head blown off. That Marra's jinxed, I tell you.'

'Jinxed?'

'Everything he touches turns to dust. Ain't that right?' he called to his brother. 'Marra's riding high now, but he won't be up there for long, I betcha. It's happened before, it'll happen again. Antonio Marra? I wouldn't shake his hand for fear of catching the pox!'

Cangio recalled what the clerk of court had told him.

'Wasn't he in trouble with the law a while back?'

'It wouldn't surprise me,' Manlio said. 'Fiddling the books, fiddling the weights and measures, fiddling his taxes. Fiddling . . . that's Antonio Marra for you. That, and worse, if you ask me.'

'What could be worse?'

'Someone reckoned that he was . . . *planting*.'

Manlio said the word as if it burnt his tongue.

'Planting what?' Cangio asked him.

'The cops were all over the place,' Manlio went on, 'but nowt ever came of it.'

'What was he growing?' Cangio insisted. 'Cannabis?'

The brothers looked at one another, then shook their heads and shrugged their shoulders, like puppets being jerked by the same string.

'Talking of mysteries,' Manlio said, reaching for a jam jar on a shelf. 'What do you make of these, then?'

Cangio held the jar up to the light.

It contained two small golden tubes.

'Fag ends,' Manlio said. 'We found them on our land one morning. Not far from where your mate's body was found, as a matter of fact, though this was ages back. We'd never seen nothing like them before. Nor since, for that matter.'

Cangio examined the contents of the jar more closely.

There was a faded blue symbol printed on the cigarette paper.

'Can I borrow these?' he asked.

'You can have them,' Manlio Pastore said. 'I should have thrown them out a long time ago. I just put them away in the jar, then forgot about them.'

'When did you find them?'

Manlio screwed his face up, thinking. 'What was it, Teo, two years back?'

'More or less,' said Teo Pastore.

Around the time of Marzio's strange sightings, Cangio thought.

Teo Pastore let out a strangled laugh.

'Maybe them's the fags that elves smoke,' he said.

TWENTY-ONE

The office was lit by candles giving off more smoke than light.

Marra stared across the Ouija board, fear gripping his chest like a tightening rope.

Maria Gatti's eyes rolled up and disappeared inside her skull. When she wasn't playing the medium, those coal black eyes were her best feature. Now they looked like marbles made of dull white glass.

Like a witch in a kids' cartoon, he told himself, though it was no joking matter.

He knew how seriously Maria took her spirits. It wasn't just a question of turning over the tarot cards and telling him what they meant, or didn't mean. Not tonight. Tonight, she was planning to ask someone for help. Some spirit of hers, she said.

A special one.

Maria said they had to go further. *Another step on the road to enlightenment*, that was what she had said. This spirit of hers could help him.

He didn't care who answered his questions. He only wanted to know what to do for the best. *Had* to know. He'd decided already more or less, but he wanted Maria and her spirit to tell him he was doing the right thing.

He glanced down at the Ouija board.

Maria had drawn it herself, and she was no artist. If he hadn't known her, he might have laughed and told her to stop fucking about.

She was mumbling over the symbols, one finger pressed down on a silver coin.

Thank God they were alone in the building. Simone and Ettore were in Rome on business. There was no one else, just him and her.

A shiver shook his shoulders. The spooky set-up, the pong of perfumed candle wax, the tight knot in his guts, the sight of Maria in a trance – it was all beginning to get to him.

'Any luck?' he whispered.

She didn't answer straight away, and, when she did, it didn't sound like her.

'We are not alone,' she said in a wheezy, high-pitched groan.

The silver coin beneath her forefinger made a sudden jerk across the Ouija board.

Slowly, she moved her head from side to side.

'Touch my hand,' she moaned. 'Make contact.'

He had to stop himself from pulling back. Maria's hand was slick with sweat, her flesh as cold and lumpy as a frozen turkey's. Is she scared, too, he wondered. Who could be more frightening, he asked himself, the dead souls Maria knew, or the . . .

The silver coin slid away across the table, pulling his hand

and Maria's with it, dragging him forward in his seat. It moved one way, then back again, and finally it settled on top of a letter.

She'd moved it, hadn't she?

He stretched his fingers along the back of her hand, pressed down on her finger. Maria's fingernail touched the silver coin and something like an electric shock went through him. Before he could make any sense of it, the coin was off again, moving this way and that, pulling their hands as if it had got them tied by a leash. He tried to pull away, but he couldn't. The silver coin kept darting left, then right, then back again, as if it didn't know its way round the Ouija board.

Maria groaned, said something. A letter, a number, then something else he didn't catch. Then off they went, shooting around the board again too fast for him to take it all in.

He looked up, and a word hissed out her lips like a dying breath.

'*Rage* . . .' she said, as the silver coin settled at the centre of the board. She pulled her hand away and said in her own voice: 'It's so fucking angry, Antò.'

Marra shifted in his chair. 'This spirit of yours—'

'It isn't *him*,' she whispered. 'I don't know who this is. Or what it wants . . .'

Maria opened her mouth to speak again, but no words came out, just a low, hollow, rumbling sound, and the surface of the Ouija board went misty, blurry, as if a cloud of fog had come between them.

He hoped to Christ she was taking the mick. That's what came of trusting his secrets to a nutcase. He should have known better. Maria Gatti was just a silly slag who looked and dressed like the weirdo she liked to think she was. The sooner it was over, the sooner she was out of the building, the better he would feel.

If only the ghost would say something useful.

There might be better ways of doing it, after all; easier ways he hadn't thought of. Ways where the risks were less. Some good argument that would convince them to get off his back and leave him alone.

'Ask him what I ought to do,' he said.

Maria's hand came down hard on his fingertips, crushing them against the silver coin and the Ouija board. 'This is different,

Antò,' she whispered, her eyes wide open, staring at him. 'This one . . . he doesn't *want* to help you.'

'Doesn't?' he said. 'Or can't?'

Maria didn't rise to the challenge.

Her eyes rolled up into her head again, and a nasty gurgling, hawking sound erupted deep down in her throat. There was no mist this time, but he felt a shiver go through him all the same.

'What do you wish to say?' she said, but not to him.

She was speaking in that strange wheezy voice again. It cracked in the middle, as if she couldn't manage to say long words, big sentences.

The coin started moving of its own accord, darting from letter to letter, pausing just an instant before it headed to the next one. Antonio Marra felt dizzy, trying hard to concentrate but unable to take in each letter or make sense of how it was moving, confused by the rapidity of it all, the sudden stopping and starting.

'M-A-K-E M-E W-H-O-L-E,' Maria spelled out.

'Make me whole? What the hell's it on about?'

'Ask him yourself,' Maria groaned, pointing at the coin in the centre of the board.

He didn't want to touch the coin, but what choice did he have? As Maria's finger pressed down on his, it was as if a race had started. The silver coin started zigging and zagging across the table, taking them with it, Maria hardly able to say a letter out loud before they went shooting off to the next one.

'C-R- . . .' Maria said, her voice getting weaker and weaker as they worked through the alphabet, gasping for breath as she pronounced the last two letters. '. . . T-H.'

CRUEL DEATH.

Which death was the spirit on about?

'Who is it?' he said, his heart pounding like a jackhammer, as if it might come bursting out of his chest. 'Is it Marzio Diamante?'

'It isn't him,' Maria said.

He felt relieved for an instant, then panic swept over him. He wanted to get up and run, but his legs felt like two lead weights, his hands were trembling, he felt light-headed.

If it wasn't Marzio . . .

'Get rid of him,' he hissed. 'Maybe yours won't come while this one's hanging round.'

Were ghosts like people at a supermarket checkout, waiting their turn while the customer in front paid his bill?

'I can't,' she said, and she sounded scared. 'He won't go away.'

Marra wiped his damp left hand on his jacket.

'Ask him what he wants . . .'

The silver coin shot across the table, dragging his finger with it, pulling him left and right, this way and that way, as Maria made out the words. Then the coin shot back to the centre of the board, and let go of his finger. It might sound stupid, but that was how it felt. One instant, he was fixed there, like a pin to a magnet, the next, the magnet had released him.

'Blood,' she said. 'It wants your blood.' Her voice was back to normal now, though there was a tremor in it. She sat there staring at him over the Ouija board.

'Did you . . . see it, Antonio?'

Noises in the room that he had never noticed before – the water pipes, the woodworm in his desk, the rattle of a glass pane in the wind blowing down from the mountains – sounded so loud and so threatening, he wanted to plug his ears and shut them out.

'Did you?' he shot back.

She looked down at the Ouija board, refusing to meet his eyes.

'What was it, Maria? Tell me!'

She shook her head, didn't speak at once. 'I . . . don't . . . know . . .'

'What the hell is that supposed to mean?' he shouted, losing it.

Maria placed her hand on his. It felt like the hand of a statue – heavy, cold and lifeless. Pearls of sweat broke out on her brow and covered her forehead. She gasped for breath.

'It had no head,' she said. 'No arms, no legs. Just a blood-soaked torso.'

TWENTY-TWO

The phone call came at ten o'clock that morning.

Normally, something like that would happen at night, which meant having to deal with an irate farmer over the phone when you couldn't do a thing to help him. If the farmer phoned at the crack of dawn instead, you had to handle the anger of a man who'd seen the damage and counted the dead, while you tried to tell him why it had happened, and stop him from trying to do anything about it.

'Last night?' Cangio asked. 'What time?'

'I've no idea,' the man said calmly. 'I wasn't here.'

It was hard for Cangio to keep the surprise out of his voice. 'You left them alone on the mountainside at night?'

'No, no,' the man said. 'I left my man and five watchdogs.'

Cangio would have liked to know more, but the farmer came to the point straight away. 'Can you come over now?' he said. 'I need you to file your report with the local police before I can put in my insurance claim.'

It took him twenty minutes to drive down from the ranger station near the summit of Monte Coscerno to Sant'Anatolia di Narco, then turn right on the Valnerina road and follow the river north towards the spot where Marzio Diamante's body had been found in the woods above Vallo di Nera.

It was the second time he had been called to the area in the last week. And yet, there was clearly no connection between what had happened last night and the fact that Marzio had been murdered there not long before. The farmer had arranged to meet him at the iron bridge that spanned the River Nera. As Cangio turned off the main road, he saw a man on the far side of the bridge, a wooden staff in one hand, a black cigar in the other.

He pulled the car over onto the grass verge, and got out. '*Signor* Tulli?'

The man held out his hand. 'Tommaso Tulli.'

'Sebastiano Cangio.'

Tulli held onto his hand with a strong grip, and didn't let go immediately. 'The ranger who likes wolves? I've heard about you,' he said.

'Good things, I hope?'

Tulli took the cigar from his lips and crushed it beneath his boot. 'They sounded OK yesterday,' he said. 'Today, I'm not so sure.'

He turned away on a path that followed the curving meander

of the River Nera through lush green meadows. The rippling chalk stream was renowned for its transparency and for its rainbow trout.

'This is my land,' Tulli told him, waving his hand across the landscape, taking in everything from the river on the right to where the woods began on the slope of the hill which would soon become Mount Bacugno. It seemed indecent to own such a vast tract of such immense beauty. 'The damned police have been trouncing all over it for the last few days, but even they couldn't have guessed that this was going to happen.'

They passed a weeping willow which trailed in the trout stream, and the scene came into view, the green meadow littered with pale white corpses which were spattered with blood. A full scale massacre, thirty carcases, or maybe more. Dead sheep, throats gouged, stomachs ripped open. From an ethologist's point of view, there was a lot to admire in what he saw. It was the lethal efficiency of the attack that was so remarkable. So much damage, so efficient and remorseless.

It had probably been done in ten minutes, or less.

'How many sheep are we talking about?' he asked.

'Yesterday, there were ninety-two. I've found seven survivors so far. It isn't the first time this has happened to me, but I didn't have so many to lose back then.'

Cangio looked around the meadow and did a quick count. 'Where are the other corpses?'

Tommaso Tulli pointed towards the woods. 'The way I figure it, the devils must have circled down to the river before they launched the attack. The sheep were closed inside hurdles and the dogs should have been on guard.'

'Should have been?'

'They were locked up in the kennels.'

'Who was watching over them, then?'

Tulli cleared his throat, then spat. 'A right good-for-nothing,' he said. 'I gave him a job and thought I was doing him a favour. Look what comes of it! He gets himself drunk, forgets to let the bloody dogs out, then sleeps all night while a pack of wolves wipes out my entire flock, more or less!'

'Where is he?' Cangio asked, hoping to get some idea of when the attack had taken place.

'I sent him packing,' Tommaso Tulli said. 'I even paid him, fool that I am!'

'So, what did he tell you?'

Tulli grunted, though it might have been a bitter laugh. 'Not much. He was . . . befuddled, let's say. He hadn't shifted from the hut all night.' Tulli pointed to a small stone building on the riverbank. 'Slept right through it, said he hadn't heard a thing!'

Cangio knelt down beside a carcase, a mature ewe with a large swollen belly. 'When were you expecting them to lamb?'

'Seven or eight weeks,' Tulli said. 'Many of them were carrying. Apart from the loss of the sheep, I intend to claim for the loss of the lambs, as well. That's why I need your report.'

Cangio placed both hands on the swollen belly of the sheep and pressed. He felt the dead-weight movement inside the corpse. 'If that man of yours had done his job and saved some of the ewes,' he said, 'you might have cut your losses come lambing time.'

'A fat hope now,' Tulli said, as Cangio moved on to the next carcase. 'If you wanted proof that wolves are killing machines, here's the evidence.'

'It's their nature,' Cangio explained. 'Wolves are predators, the important thing is to give them nothing to prey on. The park is full of boar, and there's a healthy population of deer. That amount of food keeps them happy as a rule, and it maintains the natural balance. Still, an untended flock of sheep is an invitation to a feast.'

'I don't see much sign of feasting,' Tulli said sharply. 'They didn't kill because they were hungry. Why the authorities had to go and reintroduce wolves and bears in the park has always been a mystery to me. We spent centuries killing them off, and now we want to bring them back again. It beats me, I can tell you.'

Cangio moved on to the next ewe.

The fleece was streaked with bloody claw marks where a wolf had leapt on the animal's back and dragged it down, a jagged red hole where the throat had been ripped away.

'In the past when food was scarce,' Cangio said, 'they killed whatever came along, surviving on the meat for as long as it lasted. Now there's more fresh food stock available, but that changes nothing. They kill whenever the opportunity presents itself. The survival instinct kicks in, and they slaughter everything in sight. You're lucky any survived, Signor Tulli. Someone must have frightened them off. If it wasn't your herdsman, it was you, I imagine?'

'I heard the noise and came running. I grabbed the shotgun from the hut and let off half a dozen cartridges, but I didn't manage to hit one, unfortunately.'

Cangio stood up. He didn't like the role that he was going to have to play.

'Wolves are a protected species,' he said. 'If you had killed one, you would have been in trouble. I'm here to protect you, of course, but I have to protect the wolves as well.'

Tommaso Tulli made that grunting laugh again. 'The rest of the flock is scattered all over the hillside,' he said. 'Dead, it goes without saying.'

'You should get a trailer, call for help and start collecting the carcases fast. Otherwise, they'll be back tonight for the feast that you were talking about.'

Tulli lit another cigar. 'I've got people coming to help me,' he said, and shook his head. 'You know, I'd happily sacrifice a sheep or two each season to keep them happy, but you can't make bargains with wolves. Do they have to slaughter the whole damned flock?'

'They don't know where their next meal's coming from,' Cangio said. 'You can't really blame them, can you? How many wolves did you see?'

Tulli blew out a cloud of smoke. 'Six or seven. There may have been more in the woods, of course. I fired and they scarpered.'

Cangio was there for another two hours, his notebook out, working slowly through the slaughtered sheep, keeping a tally of how many ewes were carrying lambs. In the meantime, the farmer's friends and helpers began to arrive, including the Pastore brothers and a few other men that Cangio recognised, offering a hand with the collection of the carcases. It was a grisly, unpleasant business, but it had to be done.

There were times when Cangio's love of wolves was sorely tested.

And there was worse to come.

The pack had attacked the herd from the river, driving the sheep so wild with fright that they had broken down the enclosure fence and scattered into the woods, where they were even more vulnerable. The carcase gatherers were up in the woods, not far from where the truffle reserves of the Pastore brothers and Antonio Marra began, when one of the men came over, carrying something in his hands.

'Hey, Ranger, I just found this,' he said.

He held up a mud-caked piece of bone containing half a dozen teeth.

To Cangio it looked like a human jaw.

TWENTY-THREE

*H*oly *shit!*

Had he thought it, or had he said it out loud?

Antonio Marra looked nervously around the barber's shop.

Nobody was staring at him, asking *what was up, Antò.*

His nerves were getting the better of him, that was the problem. He was thinking things, sometimes talking out loud to himself. One day he was going to get himself in trouble, saying the wrong things to the wrong people.

The wrong people?

He looked up quickly. Scissors kept on snipping, electric razors went on humming like busy little bees, the quiet exchanges of conversation between the barbers and their customers went on interrupted.

No one had heard him.

He was next in line for a trim, but two other men – faces that he vaguely recognised without being able to put a name to – were sitting on the sofas around the coffee table, reading the magazines and the daily papers.

He scanned the tiny newspaper article again. It was tucked away at the bottom of the sheet on the local news page, but an article all the same. And the worst thing of all, his name was in it. If any of his closer associates had been visiting the barber's that day, they would definitely have asked him about it.

Thank God for small mercies.

'The small Mercedes, Antonio?' Rolando asked, his scissors freezing in mid-air, raising his head, looking over his shoulder. 'You thinking of getting one of them? The new Class A's a load of crap, they say. No acceleration, lousy suspension. The Class C's one helluva motor, on the other hand . . .'

Next thing, the barbershop was alive with the talk of cars.

Antonio Marra's eyes drifted down to the bottom of the page again.

WOLF ATTACK IN VALNERINA, the title read.

He might have laughed out loud, but he didn't. There were wolves in Valnerina, all right! The two-legged kind . . .

'*. . . on the boundary near the Pastore and Marra truffle reserves. Eighty-five sheep, half of them lambing ewes, were massacred by a pack of wolves, the carcases strewn all over the valley and the hillside.*'

A wolf attack was no great surprise.

It was the next bit that had stunned him.

'*Assistant Park Ranger, Sebastiano Cangio, was at the scene supervising the clean-up operation when a shocking discovery was made. A human jaw with six teeth was found among the animal bones. When asked for an opinion, the ranger said . . .*'

'No fucking comment!'

'I'm with you there all the way, Antò,' Rolando said, razor poised above his customer's throat. 'I wouldn't drive that Alpina Coupè if you paid me.'

Jesus, Antonio Marra told himself quietly, *there must be some way out of this mess.*

He reached for his phone.

Simone Candelora and his sidekick, Ettore, were in Ferentillo that morning, something to do with another financial investment they had made.

TWENTY-FOUR

Cristina di Marco seemed too young and pretty to be a forensic pathologist.

Decked out in a white lab-coat and blue Dr Scholl's rubber clogs, she looked as if she might have graduated just the other day. Giulio Brazzini, an old friend from university days, had told him about her the night before on the phone. *Dottoressa* di Marco had taught a module for senior murder squad officers that Brazzini had attended at La Sapienza, part of the university in Rome the year before.

'Watch your step,' Brazzini had warned him. 'Cristina's a busy lady. Just ask her what you want to know, then get out fast. And remember, she doesn't have to tell you a thing, so turn on the charm, OK?'

She didn't give him a chance to turn on anything as she stepped out into the corridor and caught his eye. 'Sebastiano Cangio? The friend of Giulio Brazzini? I'm not sure that's a recommendation,' she said.

Brazzini had told him to be waiting outside room thirty-four at a quarter past nine. Cangio had arrived at a quarter to nine, and now it was a quarter to ten. He'd been tempted to knock, but hadn't wanted to interrupt whatever she might be doing.

'Thank you for seeing me.'

'Giulio didn't give me the chance to say no. He said I'd find you waiting at my door, and here you are. So, what can I do for you?'

He'd been pondering how to introduce the subject gently for the best part of an hour.

'I reported the jawbone found in Valnerina,' he said straight out.

Cristina di Marco tilted her head and looked at him. 'That was a surprise, I bet.'

She glanced towards a machine in the corridor. 'Do you fancy coffee?' she said. 'I've been here since seven o'clock this morning. I'm dying for a shot of caffeine. It's not the best blend in the world, but it does the job.'

Cangio put his hand in his pocket, searching for change. 'Let me.'

'Forget it,' she said, holding up a key on a chain. 'This is one of the perks of office. Without free coffee and lots of it, they know we wouldn't get much work done.'

Giulio had led him to expect a man-eating ogress, but Ms di Marco was quite the opposite. She seemed chatty, ready and willing to humour him. At that moment a bell rang, and suddenly the corridor was full of students who were pouring out of lectures.

'We'll be safer in my lab,' she said, handing him a plastic cup, ordering up another cup of coffee for herself. 'Students are wonderful, but wouldn't the university be a better place without them.'

'Surely, you don't see so many?' he said, as they crossed the corridor against the flow, and she unlocked the door to room thirty-four.

'You'd be surprised. I've just had ten medical students watching me do a post-mortem for the last hour and a half. At least no one threw up today!' she said, closing the door, and turning the key again. 'Safety precautions,' she said. 'This door must be kept locked at all times. I'd much prefer to work in a police forensic unit, to be honest, but . . . well, this job came up and I applied for it. A job's a job in this day and age. You don't say no, do you?'

Cangio smiled, thinking of Lori. 'I know what you mean,' he said. 'I was stuck in a place I couldn't stand, doing a job I hated, but the money was good and I needed it.'

Cristina sipped her coffee, her eyes on his. 'Which place? Which job?'

'Selling flats in London.'

'You didn't like London?' she asked incredulously. 'That's a new one!'

'I had a bedsit the size of a prison cell. I can't stand pubs, and I don't like burgers and chips. And worst of all, there are no wolves in England.' He held up a finger to stop the question he knew was coming. 'Wolves are my thing. I'm an ethologist. That's what I do in the national park. I'm monitoring three packs, and one of them massacred that herd of sheep. That was where the jaw bone you're working on came to light.'

'Have a seat,' she said, as she sat down on a stool beside a workbench.

He looked around the room, spotted a row of similar stools lined up against the far wall next to a steel frame holding six man-sized steel trays and a movable gurney. Everything was bright and spotlessly clean, even the dissected corpse that lay in orderly pieces on the tray that she had been using that morning.

'You've been busy,' he said, looking away.

'An unclaimed body,' she said. 'We get one now and then before they're buried at public expense. This fellow was a drug pusher and drugs user. Seeing the effects tends to frighten off students who might be tempted to experiment.'

She drained her coffee, put down her cup, then pursed her lips. 'I shouldn't be talking to you about a specific case, you realise that, don't you? Giulio should never have told you to get in touch with me. Officially, I am gathering evidence for the procurator's office here in Perugia, so I can't say much at all. If you want to run some ideas by me, I'm prepared to listen, though. What would Giulio say if you told him that I wouldn't help you?'

'I'll tell him you were as sweet as apple pie,' Cangio said.

She smiled again, though the smile was a little frostier this time.

'The *carabinieri* literally dropped a sack of bones on my desk. They just hand over the material and want it classified. Let me show you,' she said, taking a large cardboard archival box from a shelf and removing the lid. Cangio read the label: the date of the find, the place where it had occurred, and nothing else. Then he leant over and looked into the box.

'Apart from the jawbone, there are bits of ribs, plus various other odds and ends. I thought it was someone's idea of a joke at first. I think they'd like to catch us out if they could. Some of these fragments are human, as you know, but not all of them. I'd have made a guess at a deer or a boar, but as you mentioned wolves, I reckon I can safely narrow it down to sheep.'

'But the jawbone *is* human?'

'Oh, yes,' she said, taking two pieces of bone from the box, and holding one of them up to the light. 'The human bones are easy to recognise from the way they've been severed. Can you see the difference here? This one is from a sheep. It has teeth marks three or four centimetres in depth, wide at the top, pointed at the tip.'

'Those are typical wolf bites,' Cangio said. 'A healthy young male, three or four years old. I may even know him personally.'

Cristina di Marco laughed. 'I should have asked Giulio for *your* phone number. You could have saved me some time by classifying the animal parts.'

Cangio smiled back at her. 'Any time,' he said.

She held his gaze for a moment or two, then picked up the other bone.

'Now, have a look at this piece.'

Cangio edged closer to the table, his shoulder brushing against hers.

'It looks like part of a scapula,' he said, staring hard at an angular flap of stained bone that looked like a dried brown mushroom. 'This one doesn't belong to a sheep. It's too big.'

'It's human,' she said, leaning closer. 'Can you see how it's been broken?'

He was aware of her perfume now, a delicate trace of *eau de toilette*.

'Sheared off with one clean chop,' he said.

'A sharp implement with a cutting edge, probably steel. Hacked to bits, I'd say, though he was certainly dead when the dismembering took place. A small mercy! We don't have much of the skeleton, so it will be necessary to extend the search area if the police decide to follow up on the case.'

'But we do have pieces of an unidentified corpse.'

She stared back at him, amusement twinkling in her dark brown eyes.

'"Unidentified" is not a scientific description,' she said lightly. 'Bones can tell us a lot about the person that they once belonged to. They can't give you a name, of course, but they may indicate how old the person was, the sort of life they may have led, and, finally – and this is the bit you're really interested in, I imagine – roughly where the person came from. Funnily enough, the human jawbone is one of the most useful parts of the human body in that respect. I was checking the web last night, and I came across an intriguing article, "The Determination of Ancestry from Discrete Traits of the Mandible", by a researcher from the

University of Florida. She pointed out something odd, something that I couldn't make any sense of when I was examining this jawbone yesterday.'

She raised her cup to her lips, found it empty and put it down again.

Cangio pushed his coffee cup across the table.

'I haven't touched it,' he said.

'Thanks,' she said with a Mona Lisa smile, but she didn't touch the coffee. 'Aren't you going to ask me what was odd? My first-year students would have leapt on it.'

'What couldn't you make sense of?'

'The problem with your jawbone – well, not *yours*, but this one – is that it doesn't . . . *rock*.' She looked at him and raised her eyebrows. Her brown eyes were flecked with gold. 'That doesn't sound very scientific, does it? So, let me explain. When I first removed the mandible, or inferior maxillary bone, from the plastic evidence bag, and set it down on the lab bench, it lay quite flat on the surface. As a rule, a jawbone from Europe, America or Africa will gently rock if you touch it, a bit like an old-fashioned grandma's chair. The point of gravity is some-where in the middle, you see. But not all human jaws behave the same way. Indeed, the mandible of a person from the Far East tends to sit square and flat on a solid surface. That was the first thing that I noticed. The jaw bone didn't rock, as I said, so I had to ask myself if I was dealing with a non-Italian jaw . . .'

As she spoke, her manner became distracted and remote, as if she were going through the thought process once again.

'What conclusion did you reach?' Cangio asked.

She shook her head. 'It isn't so simple,' she said. 'Without dragging you into the complex world of dental morphology, I can tell you what assumptions I was able to make about the teeth that are still attached to the jaw. Judging by their size and shape, and the wear that is evident, especially regarding the shovel-shaped incisors, I would say beyond any reasonable doubt, that this particular jawbone belonged to a healthy Asian man aged somewhere between forty and fifty years old. Now, as the vast majority of Asians are ethnically Chinese . . .'

Cangio sat back and took in what she had just told him.

'You're saying that the jawbone once belonged to a Chinese man?'

Cristina di Marco shook her forefinger at him. 'Officially, I haven't told you anything. We're just friends having coffee together.' She raised his coffee cup to him, and took a sip. 'Cold, but coffee nonetheless,' she said.

Should he invite her out to dinner, he wondered.

Again the ghost of Loredana hovered over his head.

'If you'll excuse me,' she said, before he had committed himself, 'I have to prepare for my lecture.'

As Cangio left room thirty-four, a question was rattling around in his head.

Why had a middle-aged Chinese man with good teeth been chopped to pieces in an Umbrian national park?

TWENTY-FIVE

'What's the problem, Antò?'

Simone Candelora already knew the answer.

The little prick was so see-through, he was transparent. The minute he got to the adventure park in Ferentillo, Marra's big brown eyes had lit on his, and stuck there fast. Then they'd started to water up, as if Marra was going to cry, reminding Simone of a pup he'd had as a kid, a little black mongrel called Mutt that would follow him around all day. Marra looked like Mutt on a bad day, just begging for a kick.

Antonio was rubbing his hands together like someone getting ready to confess his sins. Then he clutched his nose between his thumb and forefinger, gave it a tug and let out an audible sniff. 'I've been having a serious think, Simone,' he said, delivering his speech. 'About the future, like. It, er . . . it might be better for you, as well.'

'Better for us,' he said to Ettore. 'Hear that, Ettò? Our mate here's driven all this way to tell us what's been rumbling around in his head. That's polite, it really is. No sooner did he have this little *think* than up he charges, bursting to tell us what it's all about. He's the ideal partner in my book.' He turned back to Marra. 'OK, partner. Let's hear it. What've you been thinking?'

Antonio Marra licked his lips. 'It's in all the papers,' he said. 'Some wolves have gutted a herd of sheep near my . . . near *our* reserve. A right mess by the sound of it.'

'So what?' Simone grinned at him. 'Were those sheep yours?'

Marra didn't answer him. 'The papers said they'd found some . . . bones. Human bones, it seems. From years ago. The wolves must have dug 'em up. You know, close to where the ranger was killed. The police were there again.'

'Were they your wolves, Antò?' Ettore said, which made Simone laugh.

Sheep and bones were only the half of what was going on in that prat's mind, Simone reckoned. Antonio Marra had something else on his plate. And what could it be, if not what Arnaldo Capaldi had warned him about the other day at the hotel? He could only hope the little shit hadn't signed anything, or gone over Capaldi's head and spoken to someone higher up in the bank.

Mutt needed kicking, good and proper.

'Come and see what we've been up to,' Simone said. 'Marra Truffles isn't the only firm that we've put money into. Everywhere you look in Umbria, there's opportunity going to waste, cash going down the drain. It's all a question of management. Look around you, Antò. This one here's a potential goldmine.'

He laid a hand on Marra's shoulders and saw his eyes flash wide, like someone who'd been sleepwalking suddenly waking up, as they started walking out onto the narrow metal bridge that crossed the limestone gorge, with its sixty-metre drop, sheer cliffs rising up on either side and the river rushing down below.

'Where are we going?' Marra asked.

Terror. Undiluted terror. That's what he could see on Marra's face.

And that was what he wanted to see.

'Just a short walk. What a view!'

They'd been in Terni that morning, signing papers with the owner of the adventure park, when Marra had phoned him, wanting to meet up straight away. Lunch in Vallo di Nera, dinner that night in Spoleto? No way, Marra said, it couldn't wait.

In the end, they'd agreed to meet in Ferentillo at midday.

The adventure park was a bit run-down, but that was fine. They had planning permission, a building license; all they had to do was decide which bits to develop. Laundering dirty bank-notes was easier in some circumstances than others. The bungee jumping, for instance, out there in the middle of nowhere. Who was ever going to check on that? One paying customer a day, or none at all, you could write up a thousand receipts, then burn the tickets at the end of the day. Pay the taxes, that was ten thousand euro washed clean. Do it every day for a year, and you were talking serious money. Don Michele was behind them all they way. 'I like it when my boys have bright ideas,' he had said.

'We're gonna call it Thrillsville,' he said to Marra as they stopped in the centre of the gorge. All around them air and light, with just the slender metal bridge between them and the abyss.

'Ettore, give him a hand, will you?'

It was a bit like helping a condemned man onto the gallows.

An extension had been welded onto the bridge, a viewing platform, or something of the sort. Marra didn't want to step out there, but he knew he had to, knew he couldn't say no.

Next thing, he was staring into space.

Simone waved his hand through the air. 'See those rocks, Antò? You ever been rock climbing? What a thrill! People pay plenty to learn how to do it. Little kids, teenagers, mums and dads who fancy doing something a bit different on a Sunday afternoon.'

'People pay to do it?' Marra muttered sceptically.

'They'll pay to do anything,' Ettore said quietly over Marra's left shoulder. 'You'd be surprised how much they'll pay. Now, *stick 'em up!*' Ettore jabbed the harness buckle hard into the small of Marra's back.

The truffle merchant's hands shot into the air.

Ettore dropped the straps over his shoulders, stepped around quickly to snap the buckle shut.

'What's this?' Marra said, pulling at the straps, which were tight around his chest.

'Safety gear,' Ettore told him. 'Just in case you slip.'

'*Thinking*, Antò. *Serious thinking*, you said.' Simone was leaning so close, he could smell Marra's breath. 'About what, in particular?'

'You know,' Marra said quickly. 'The company. Our arrange-ment   '

'You want to rip up the contract, something like that? Getting out of a contract can be costly, can't it, Ettò?'

Ettore hissed into Marra's ear. 'No telling how much it might cost, Simò.'

'I . . . I'll give you the company,' Marra said, hands together, begging almost. 'Marra Truffles. Lock, stock and—'

'What about our investment? Good faith, and suchlike? What about the interest?'

Marra blinked hard at him. 'You can have it all,' he said. 'Everything. The house, the car, the . . . the . . . I've got some savings stashed away in Switzerland.'

Simone shrugged, flashed a grin, nodded at Ettore, then stared in Antonio Marra's eyes. 'We can't get along without you, Antò. You know the business. We're just the money men. The backers, right?'

Marra was desperate now. 'You don't need me,' he said. 'Maria was saying—'

'Maria Gatti? You shagging that piece, Antò?' Ettore was laughing. 'Fuck me, I didn't think you had it in you.'

'Shut it, Ettore.' Simone narrowed his eyes, stared at Marra. 'Have you been talking about the business with her?'

Marra looked down at his shoes, didn't say a word.

'Have you told her what we're doing?'

'No. Honest. I haven't . . .'

His voice was more of a whimper now. Just like Mutt when the dog wanted feeding.

That was when Candelora laid both hands on Marra's chest and pushed him backwards.

It was worse than a nightmare.

This was real.

His hands grabbed air, his feet kicked air.

He tried to scream, but all the air had gone out of lungs.

He saw two heads leaning over the bridge, watching him fall.

Pinpricks disappearing down the wrong end of a telescope.

Then he lost them, the metal strip of the bridge getting thinner by the moment, the rock walls rushing past on either side. Not racing upwards, though that was how it seemed. It was him that was rocketing downwards, hurtling down towards the rocks and the river at the bottom of the gorge.

He closed his eyes, his breath came back and he did scream then, the wind swooshing all around him, pulling at his face, his hair, his clothes, the harness tightening beneath his crotch and thighs, ripping at his armpits.

The harness.

Had Ettore locked it?

The cord was like a wriggling snake above his head, until it started to straighten, pulling taut in a stark black line against the clear blue sky. His ears popped and he heard a loud noise – a *twang* like a guitar string snapping, then a loud *boing*, and suddenly he was shooting back up towards the bridge again.

Ettore had locked it.

This time.

TWENTY-SIX

Foligno was a town that Cangio tried to avoid.

It was flatter than a compact disc, while he loved Umbria for the mountains.

Bicycles darted left and right, more dangerous than cars, and no one bothered with anything so trivial as a bicycle bell.

'What are we doing here?' Loredana asked him, as they walked across the main square. 'This place really makes me nervous.'

She glanced up at the truncated steeple of the town hall, a stark reminder of just how big the last earthquake had been and how long it was taking to set it all to rights.

'Well . . .' he said, his mind working overtime.

Foligno was halfway to Todi, and Lori had a half-day holiday, but that was not the only reason Cangio had suggested meeting her there.

'It's *lu centru dellu munnu*,' he joked. 'That's what the locals say. Foligno's in the centre of Italy, and Italy was the centre of the ancient world.'

She glared at him. 'The centre of *my* world is where I happen to be, Seb Cangio.'

If she was thinking of Todi, the enforced separation, he tried to shake her out of it.

'With me, you mean?'

'Only if I'm the centre of your world,' she said moodily.

'OK, let's agree on that,' he said.

Had he had made a mistake to bring her there? She was jumpy. He hadn't seen her since the funeral, but she had kept her promise, phoning at eleven o'clock each night on the dot. She was worried that he might go out into the woods alone.

'I'm home,' he'd say, whenever she rang.

Last night he'd been in the park instead, popping the eye cap on his night-vision glasses, telling her he was opening a can of beer. He wasn't sure she'd believed him, but at least she didn't hound him about it. He had other things on his mind, and she knew it. One thing in particular. Who had killed Marzio?

'Where are you taking me?' she asked again.

'It's a surprise,' he said for the tenth time.

'There are surprises and . . . *surprises*,' she murmured.

'This is one of those,' he said as they turned into a side street and headed for a neon sign that read *The Szechuan*. 'Have you ever eaten here?'

She held his arm, stopped him dead in his tracks. 'Umbria's got the best food in Italy, and you are taking me to . . .'

'A Chinese restaurant.' He grinned, brushed her cheek with his lips. 'I survived on ethnic food in London. Indian, Chinese, Thai. Man liveth not on egg and chips alone,' he intoned like a clergyman. 'Trust me, Lori, you'll love it.'

The Szechuan turned out better than he had hoped and Lori had expected.

They ordered a Chinese banquet for two – wonton soup, spring rolls, beef with mangetout, chicken in black bean sauce, fried shrimp with pork – all washed down with Tsingtao beer.

Over the meal they talked about Marzio and the ongoing investigation.

He tried to keep it low key, grateful that she didn't press him too hard for details.

Lori had been phoning Linda every day. 'She's been interviewed by two *carabinieri*, a man and a woman. Twice, she said. Have they spoken to you, as well?'

'They're speaking to everyone,' he said.

'But I mean to say, after what happened to you the last time?'

'They don't think organised crime is involved.'

'No?' Loredana was wide-eyed, staring at him as if she couldn't believe what she was hearing. 'So, who do they think *is* responsible?'

'I'm sure they'll tell us when they've made up their minds,' he said.

He ordered ice cream for Lori, another Tsingtao beer for himself.

When the sweet arrived, Lori was disappointed.

'This is Italian ice cream,' she whispered. '*Stracciatella* . . . Still, I suppose it must be hard for them to find the right ingredients here in Italy. I mean to say, bamboo shoots, spices, and all those funny vegetables. They seemed so fresh and tasty, too. And the rice isn't the same as ours. Where do think they come from, Seb?'

It was a smart question, though he didn't realise it straight off.

'There must be Chinese shops,' he said, 'wholesalers, suppliers, that kind of thing.'

When the waiter came to see if everything was all right, Cangio decided to ask him. After all, it was time to start working around to the question that had brought him there in the first place.

The waiter turned out to be the owner of the restaurant, and he was happy to fill them in on the details. His name was Heng Lu, he said, and he had been born in Szechuan province, southwest China. The rice and noodles came in plastic packets. 'Just like Italian spaghetti,' he said with a grin. The meat and fish were from the local supermarket. The beer, spices and vegetables were from a Chinese superstore outside Rome that did express deliveries.

'You speak excellent Italian,' Cangio said. 'How long have you been in Italy?'

'Nearly twenty years,' the man said proudly. 'My kids were born here. Not *here* exactly. One in Rome, the other one in Florence. Then I decided to open a restaurant of my own. We've been in Foligno eight years now.'

The eight years were rubbing off on him; he pronounced *Fuligno* like a local.

There were only a couple of other customers left in the restaurant, and Heng Lu seemed to be in no hurry to get rid of them. He was in his late forties or early fifties, Cangio guessed from the deep lines etched in his brow and at the sides of his nose, black hair swept straight back from his forehead. Cangio couldn't help but study the man's square-cut jaw, wondering whether it would rock if you set it down on a table. For one unfaithful moment, he imagined the pretty pathologist sitting on the other side of the table taking a careful look at the Chinese man's jaw.

'My oldest boy is seventeen. He'll be going to university next year. Have you got any kids?' Heng Lu asked, which threw Loredana into a flurry. This was the kind of talk she got from her mother, who seemed to think that a woman of twenty-seven should be tied to the kitchen sink and coming up for her second child.

'We aren't married,' she said, her mood much better than before. She had enjoyed the meal, and the fact that the police believed the 'Ndrangheta were not involved in Marzio's murder had set her mind at rest.

'No one gets married these days,' the Chinese man said.

Cangio smiled at that, and so did Loredana, though her smile was slower in coming.

'Is there a large Chinese community in Umbria?' Cangio asked him.

This was one of the things that he had come to Foligno to find out.

Lori narrowed her eyes and fixed him with a stare; she was not fooled by his attempts to be casual.

'Not so many,' Heng Lu told him. 'There are twenty-odd in Foligno. Slightly more in Terni and Perugia.'

'I work in the national park,' Cangio told him, 'and I found something very unusual the other day. I'm curious to know if you can tell me what it is. I thought it might be Chinese. We have quite a few tourists from the Far East these days.'

Heng Lu spread his hands wide, and shrugged his shoulders. *What's the problem*, he seemed to be saying, gesturing like an Italian.

Cangio took a piece of paper from his pocket, unfolded it and handed it over. He had scanned the symbol from the golden cigarette ends that the Pastore brothers had found, and then blown it up to maybe twenty times the size of the original.

$$蝴蝶$$

'This is a Chinese symbol for a butterfly,' Heng Lu said. 'Where did you find it?'

'It was printed on a cigarette. Like Pall Mall, or Camel.'

Cangio took a sip of beer and waited.

Heng Lu looked at the paper again, then folded it up and handed it back.

'It's not the name of a cigarette,' he said. 'It's the name of a restaurant and supermarket chain in Soho, London. One of the best. I worked in Soho for a while, so I know the place. This symbol means "Come back soon". Like the butterflies, you know? They give them free to the customers and hope they'll return.' Heng Lu laughed. 'Just think of it! Someone was in London one day, and the next thing he was smoking Chinese cigarettes in your park here in Umbria.'

Cangio saw the expression on Loredana's face.

'Surprise, surprise,' she said, reaching for her bag, as he reached for his wallet.

Out in the street, she turned on him. 'A quiet meal in Foligno with your girlfriend, eh? What the hell have Chinese cigarettes got to do with the death of Marzio Diamante?'

She was angry, and for once, he didn't know how to answer her.

TWENTY-SEVEN

Maria Gatti laid out the cards.

Every time, Moon came out with Judgement as the second card in the set of three.

The combination stank of betrayal, though who was betraying whom, she couldn't say.

Her heart was thumping painfully. It wasn't often you turned up a sequence so negative, and she still hadn't flipped the upper and lower cards that formed the cross.

She hadn't dared to turn them over, that was the truth of it.

It was a warning, all right.

And coming so soon after the evil spirit that had appeared the other night.

Maria lit a cigarette from one of the guttering candles. You weren't supposed to, but she wasn't sure where she had put the lighter. She blew smoke at the ceiling and watched the blue cloud cut through the shadows and caress the oak beams, the dancing shapes of the furniture projected by the candlelight. The shadows were part of the drama the cards created on the table, strange shapes and distortions that were never the same from one night to the next. The shadows played their part, too.

You could read whatever you liked into those, if you felt like doing it.

Antonio Marra was becoming a problem.

The Sun would decide, Judgement would decree.

Which left the Moon, the mystery which cannot be revealed . . .

She should have cut Antonio loose. He was like a kid who kept scuffing his knees but never seemed to learn the lesson. She would help him out of one hole, knowing that he'd go diving down into a deeper hole than the one he'd just climbed out of. He was lazy, careless, attracted by risks and easy profit, never able to see the danger until it was too late.

He had started coming to see her again about three months before.

Investors were pouring cash into the company, he said, turning Marra Truffles around. He'd soon be a millionaire, he said, but it made no sense. Who'd throw money into a company that wasn't worth a fart? No sane businessman would take on someone else's bad debts unless he saw an advantage in it for himself. But Marra couldn't think that far. Antonio Marra couldn't think at all.

Then something must have frightened him, because he'd started phoning more and more.

And then that *thing* had appeared during the séance.

Maria stubbed her cigarette in the ashtray.

That had really scared her. A body with no arms, no legs, no head.

And now, tonight, the tarot cards.

She found his number, pressed the button, held the phone to her ear.

The number you have dialled is not available, a metallic voice said. *Please leave a message after the beep.*

'Antonio, it's me,' she said, sorry he hadn't answered, glad at the same time. 'The tarot cards are still the same. The message is clear. Remember what I told you.' She was silent for a moment. 'Call me back as soon as you can.'

She snapped the mobile phone shut.

She tried the cards again. Twice. It was always the same.

The Moon with her disapproving frown, the third phase like the curved blade of an executioner's axe.

She turned away and opened the fridge door.

It was like pulling the stopper from a perfume bottle. The scent came billowing out in a cloud. Antonio had given her a bag of truffles instead of paying. She closed her eyes and took a deep breath.

Why did they say the Virgin Mary smelled of roses?

Roses were nothing compared to fresh truffles.

That's what Antonio had told her the first time he had asked her to read the cards for him two or three years before. Not long after that, the cops had questioned him. He'd been under pressure for a week or two, then it had all blown over. He had never told her what it was about, and she didn't want to know, if she was honest.

She picked a large truffle, and the thought of food began to push aside the tension the tarot cards had provoked. Spaghetti with truffles, washed down with what was left of the Trebbiano wine she'd uncorked the other night.

That would put her in a better mood.

She filled a saucepan with water, added salt and lit the gas, then held the truffle under the tap, rubbing it gently with an old toothbrush to remove the mud that was clinging to it. Next, she put a small frying pan on the stove, added olive oil, split a clove of garlic, then dropped it and a small red pepper into the oil. She grated the truffle as she waited for the oil to sizzle.

That was when she heard a noise.

She pushed aside the curtain; her face stared back at her in the glass.

Night was always pitch black in the mountains. The only light she could see was a farm on the far side of the valley, five or six kilometres away.

The noise could have been anything, a car on the road, or something blowing loose in the wind.

She laid the table quickly and switched on the TV. They were talking about politics. She turned down the volume. Then she snagged a strand of spaghetti with a fork, raised it to her mouth and bit into the pasta. *Al dente*. Not too hard, and not too soft. The way it should be.

She was pouring the pasta into a plastic colander when she heard the noise again.

She stopped dead, the saucepan poised over the colander, listening to the low buzz of the TV, the sound of water gurgling down the plughole.

Something out in the garden. A cat or a wolf . . .

She gave the colander a shake, then poured the spaghetti into the pan with the truffle sauce.

A rattling noise came from the door out in the hallway.

She covered the pan with a lid, stepped into the hall and stared at the door.

If anyone came to see her at home, they came by appointment.

She hadn't arranged a sitting that night.

She inched towards the door on tiptoe, then heard a footstep on the gravel. The visitor must have seen the light in the kitchen and gone to look just as she was moving into the hallway. She half smiled to herself.

'Antonio? Is that you?'

He must have heard her phone message and decided to stop by.

She slipped the chain off the door and pulled back the deadbolt, already speaking as she turned the lock. 'Were you in the area when I called you?'

'Yes,' a voice said, as she opened the door.

It didn't sound like Marra.

As the door swung back, a fist smashed into her face.

A shadow grabbed her by the throat, pushing her backwards into the kitchen.

The attacker held her down as she fell on to the table, then swept something up, splattering hot wax in her face, burning her tongue and cheeks.

The heavy metal candlestick came crashing down on her forehead.

Again and again and again.

TWENTY-EIGHT

C angio knew that he was making a mistake.

Intruding where he hadn't been invited, they were not going to like it.

Manlio Pastore had phoned him at half-past seven.

'There's cop cars up in Cerreto. *Them two* again,' he'd said in a throaty rumble. 'I thought you'd want to know.'

It might have been funny the way everyone spoke of Grossi and Esposito, but if the Regional Crime Squad had been called out, there was nothing to laugh about.

'The first house before you reach the village,' Manlio told him. 'You can't miss it.'

As he raced down the mountainside and turned onto the Valnerina road, he realised with a start what he was letting himself in for. Everything to the right of the highway was national park, while Cerreto was up on top of a mountain off to the left. It was out of his jurisdiction. Maybe they'd just tell him to get lost and go back to work.

Whatever was going on, he wanted to know.

Now, not later.

Of course, they might just be checking leads, catching up with people before they left for work, trying to clear things up.

And if they asked him what he was doing there?

He smiled for the first time that morning.

He'd tell them he was going up to Cerreto to have his breakfast. The bar in the main square served the best cappuccino in Umbria. It might be nothing, after all, just routine checks involving anyone in the area who had known Marzio.

He tried to believe it, but it wouldn't wash.

The RCS meant serious crimes.

The road up to Correto was one blind bend after another, the narrow road jutting out from the cliffside on concrete props in places. He had almost reached the top when a car flew out of a bend; a Mercedes Coupé racing downhill fast cut the corner and crossed the centre line, heading straight at him.

Cangio jammed his foot on the brake.

The driver of the Mercedes did the same. Both cars slewed and skidded, coming to a halt just inches apart, nose to nose, bumper to bumper, miraculously untouched. Two pairs of sunglasses stared out of the Mercedes, a third man, silhouetted in the light from the rear window, sitting on the bench seat behind them.

'A close shave,' Cangio muttered to himself.

The man in the back seat leant forward, saying something to the driver.

What was Antonio Marra doing up there?

Cangio slipped the gear lever into reverse and edged back from the Mercedes, his eyes fixed on the driver's dark glasses, making room to let him pass. Had the cars collided, one of them would have been hitting the ground a hundred and fifty metres below at that very moment.

An electric shock jolted through his veins.

He clenched his teeth to stop from shouting out.

It wasn't pain, or anger. It was worse. Like being pitched back into the middle of the nightmare which had troubled him for months.

He was looking into the muzzle of a gun, a finger tightening on the trigger, two dark eyes peering out at him from a full-face crash helmet. And on the killer's neck, a blue tattoo of a lizard.

He had run away to London after that experience. He had relived it in his dreams most nights, waking up in a cold sweat as he heard the metallic *click* of the empty pistol pointing at his forehead.

The driver of the Mercedes had glanced to the right, gauging the gap as he steered the big car through it, exposing his neck as he looked down into the abyss. And Cangio had spotted the lizard tattooed beneath his left ear.

The driver glanced back at him, and nodded. *No harm done.*

Cangio had to force himself to raise his thumb as the Mercedes surged away.

He watched in the rear view mirror as it disappeared around the bend, heading down into the valley. He felt as if the nightmare bullet had just hit him between the eyes. Then he began to breathe again. Was the driver the gunman he had seen at Soverato beach the summer before last? Another member of the same clan?

That tattoo was the proof.

He'd been right from the start: the enemy was back.

The 'Ndrangheta.

Had the gunman known or recognised him?

As he turned the key, revved the engine, and pulled away, another thought came into his mind. What was Antonio Marra doing in the Mercedes with them?

It wasn't far to the top. As he rounded the final bend, the road flattened out. On the right was a farmhouse at the end of a short dirt track. Two *carabinieri* vehicles were parked outside. He stopped by the side of the dirt road, then started to walk towards the trio who were gathered outside the front door.

Sustrico, Grossi and Esposito.

Tonino Sustrico saw him first. The *brigadiere* raised his chin as if to say *Ah, you're here.* He took half a dozen paces in Cangio's direction. Grossi and Esposito looked the other way, freezing him out. They were going to make him walk barefoot on sharp stones before they'd tell him what was going on.

'I was on the point of calling you,' Sustrico said 'And they say this place is off the beaten track! It's worse than High Mass in the cathedral on Christmas Day. Everyone sees you if you go, and takes notice if you don't. Who told you we were—'

Cangio changed route quickly. 'You were going to you call me?' he said

Sustrico pointed behind him with his thumb, and made a grimace. '*Those two* want to speak with you.'

Evidently, the *brigadiere* still hadn't warmed to the RCS.

'What would they want to speak to me about?'

Sustrico puffed out his cheeks. 'You'd better ask them,' he said.

A mobile CS van parked in the lee of the house told Cangio to expect the worst. Add the rest – the killer of his nightmares in a car with Antonio Marra, the presence of the hot-shot cops from Perugia – and what did you have?

'Ndrangheta.

'What's going on?' he asked.

Sustrico lowered his head. 'If the vultures are here . . .' he said, without saying any more.

'Who called them?'

'A couple of men have been working behind the house for a week, fixing metal nets to catch falling rocks. The shutters are usually open, they said. The woman gives them tea or coffee. This morning the shutters were closed. The workmen were concerned . . . for their coffee, I bet. They went to knock on the front door, found it open. I was on duty when the call came in. When I saw the mess, I had to call for *them*.' Sustrico frowned. 'A bad job all round.'

Grossi and Esposito turned towards him in that instant. They didn't make a move to greet him, standing there like a pair of defenders waiting for a dangerous free kick to be taken.

'Cangio,' Lucia Grossi said with a bemused expression. 'What a coincidence!'

'What are you doing here?' Esposito growled.

The breakfast in Cerreto story dissolved in an instant. 'A little bird,' he said.

'Which *little bird* was that?' Esposito couldn't keep the sarcasm out of his voice.

Cangio smiled. 'The woods around here are full of them. An anonymous phone call saying there were police cars in the vicinity.'

'Oh, right,' Esposito nodded. 'I nearly forgot. The king of the jungle. If anything happens in your neck of the woods, you jump straight on it. Just in case it makes the news—'

'This *is* my neck of the woods,' Cangio shot back at him. 'If anything happens, it's my job to check it out. That's what the county pays me for.'

'OK, you two, cut it out,' snapped Lucia Grossi, playing the peacemaker. 'You're here now, Cangio, and that's the important thing. We were thinking over something you said about the night your partner was found. That's why we wanted you to . . . Hang on, though. First, we'll take a peek, then hear what you've got to say about it.'

'It? What are you talking about?'

The cops exchanged a glance like two soloists getting ready to hit the opening note on cue. Without a word Lucia Grossi led him into the house.

The first thing that hit him was the smell of cat piss.

Then cats emerged from out of the gloom for an instant to stare at them, before darting away into the darkness. There were pictures, statues and figures made of metal, wood and plastic, a row of skulls the size of apples hanging on the walls. Cats. On a table in the far corner, a stuffed cat sat beneath a dusty glass dome.

'What a name!' Jerry Esposito hissed. 'Maria *Gatti* as in cats. Was she born with it, do you reckon, or was it part of the pantomime?'

Cangio bent down before the glass dome. Wild green eyes stared back at him. The animal's mouth was howling, showing sharp, pointed teeth. *Let me go, or I'll rip your eyes out!* it seemed to be screeching.

Cangio turned to Esposito. 'I imagine you know what she did?'

'Played the witch is what we hear.' Esposito clicked his tongue. 'Gives me the creeps, this place.'

'There's more to see,' Lucia Grossi added, leading Cangio into the kitchen.

It was a big room, maybe the largest in the house, a massive open fireplace on the left, a long dining table in the middle, a big stone sink on the right. The room smelled of damp and centuries of cooking. And there was something else that turned his stomach.

Blood.

Two technicians in white plastic coveralls were working by the sink, one brushing for fingerprints, the other one taking photographs.

A body was laid out on the floor, a white foot peeping out from beneath a dark green cotton shroud. A depression in the floor contained a lake of blood, while thin dark veins of blood had spread across the room, following the zigzag pattern of the tiles.

Cangio tried to imagine the body hidden beneath the cloth, but something protruding from the corpse formed a wigwam, with a pointed tent where the heart ought to be.

Grossi and Esposito seemed to be in no hurry to show him the body.

Cangio swallowed hard.

'I saw Antonio Marra going down the hill as I was coming up.'

'We sent for him,' Lucia Grossi said, 'but we didn't show him this. It wouldn't have served any purpose.'

So why are you showing me? thought Cangio.

'What's Marra got to do with it?' he asked, bending low, as if all his attention was centred on the corpse.

'Maria Gatti's phone,' Esposito replied. 'He was the last person she called.'

Cangio looked towards the sink on the far side of the large room.

His throat was dry; he would have given anything for a glass of water.

'They were long-time friends,' Esposito said.

'Marra was in a car with two men. Did they know Maria Gatti, as well?'

Cangio held his breath, expecting to be told to mind his own business.

'They were clients, apparently,' Esposito said. 'They did him a favour, drove him up here. He wasn't sure he could make it on his own when he heard the news. To say that he was in a state says little.'

'Might she and Marra have met last night?'

'He was dining out with those two men,' Lucia Grossi said.

Cangio stood up and faced her. 'They backed him up, of course.'

Lucia Grossi pursed her lips. 'Naturally. Why shouldn't they?'

'She left him a voice message,' Esposito said. 'He played it back for us.'

Cangio decided to push harder. 'I bet it didn't say much.'

'Something about the tarot cards,' the woman said. 'She'd been reading the cards for him.'

'That's what she did for a living.'

'Did she ever read the cards for you?' Lucia Grossi asked.

Esposito nodded in the direction of the kitchen table. 'That's what she was doing before someone killed her.'

Cangio turned to look.

A pack of cards had been loosely discarded, other cards laid out in the form of a cross, three exposed, two face down.

'The cards of destiny,' Esposito said.

'She was preparing dinner,' Lucia Grossi said. 'One plate, one glass, one knife and fork, a glass of wine. She was treating herself to truffles, so there must be money in the job. She wasn't afraid when someone came to the door. Whoever it was, she let the killer in.'

'Maybe someone turned up out of the blue for a reading.'

'It's possible.'

'But it wasn't Marra.'

Grossi and Esposito replied in chorus, 'Not Marra.'

Which left the thug with the lizard tattoo on his neck. Or the other man.

'So what can I tell you?' Cangio asked.

Lucia Grossi arched her eyebrows. 'When the corpse of Marzio Diamante was found, you spoke about satanic rites and ritual sacrifices.'

That threw Cangio for a moment.

Where was this leading?

'Like I told you, Marzio thought weird things were going on in the park.'

The cops swapped glances.

'You think this was a ritual killing?' Cangio asked them.

Lucia Grossi pursed her lips at him. 'That's what someone would *like* us to think.'

Should he tell them about the murder at Soverato beach, and what he thought the two men in the car with Marra might be doing in Umbria? He dismissed the idea. He knew how *these two* would react if he mentioned the 'Ndrangheta. They would accuse him of trying to derail their investigation, and get himself into the news again.

And what did he have to go on, except a tattoo of a lizard?

Jerry Esposito turned to his partner. 'Cangio's a big boy. He's been around. He's been shot, too. He won't faint like the lab guy did. Shall we show him what happened here last night?'

Lucia Grossi seemed to consider it for a moment. 'Why not?'

she said. 'If he's so keen.' She looked at Cangio, nodded when he did, then bent over, stretched out her hand and pulled away the green cotton sheet that was hiding the body.

Cangio didn't faint, but his head began to spin.

'The position of the knife is odd,' Lucia Grossi was saying. Her voice seemed to come from a long way away. 'Vertical, you see? Driven straight through the heart. Like those wooden stakes they use to kill vampires in the movies.'

A bread knife had been pushed deep into the body right between the breasts.

'She was dead when that was planted there. The head had already . . .'

Cangio blew out air and said, 'Where is the head?'

The two men dusting down the draining board moved aside like automatons, exposing the big stone kitchen sink, as Jerry Esposito said, 'Go on, take a look.'

Cangio took half a dozen paces, stared at the wall for a moment, then looked down.

Two eyes stared glassily up at him. Maria Gatti's severed head had been laid out like the Sunday joint before it went into the oven.

Three tarot cards had been carefully laid around it.

The Ace of Clubs – The Two of Cups – Death.

'When we saw this set-up—'

Lucia Grossi cut her partner off. 'Someone wants us to believe there's black magic and satanic evil behind what's going on in the national park. We were hoping you might be able to explain it to us.'

Cangio was too surprised to speak for some moments.

'What can *I* tell you?'

Esposito turned on him.

'You could start by telling us . . .'

'You are a person "informed of the facts,"' Lucia Grossi cut in, 'though you may not be aware of the full significance of the facts that you know. It's a matter of formal procedure, Cangio. We need to question you now as a potential witness. The interview will be recorded and then transcribed. If necessary, our findings will be passed on to the investigating magistrate. As you can see, we're going to be busy here for the rest of the day, but we'll be expecting you tomorrow afternoon in Perugia. At two o'clock, let's say.'

'You know the address,' Esposito said. 'Third floor."

TWENTY-NINE

'**M**urderers!'
The kick that hit the back of his knee could have come from a mule.

He collapsed like an empty sack, cracking his mouth on the rim of the toilet as he went down, a molar snapping off as it hit the porcelain. He tasted blood and spat red drool into the frothy water where he'd been peeing just a minute before.

Arriving at the factory from Maria Gatti's, they'd pulled him out of the Mercedes and marched him into the hallway, holding him up like a drunk, or a prisoner. He'd hardly been able to stand on his own two feet.

Rosanna had come running from behind the reception desk, making a fuss, but Simone Candelora had shrugged her off. 'He'll soon get over it. A bit of a shock, that's all. A dear friend who died all of a sudden.' Then his voice had hardened. '*Signor* Marra would like to be left in peace for a bit. Spread the word, will you?'

Next thing, they were in the office. Him and them. No one else in the factory would know if he was dead or alive. As they sat him down on top of his desk, that was what he thought was coming next.

They were going to snuff him.

'I've got to go,' he said. 'The bog . . . I need to pee.'

The bathroom window might be his only chance to get out of there. It was a trick he'd often used before, when someone turned up unannounced to collect a debt. If he could put a bit of distance between him and them, he could call the cops he'd spoken to at Maria's place.

'Sure, go ahead,' Candelora said, then they followed him into the toilet, stood by the door and watched him do it, so the window was a dead loss.

'You ain't pissing much for a man who's desperate,' Ettore sneered.

The bastards had killed Maria. Now, they were going to kill him, too.

That was when the first kick came.

A second kick slammed into his kidneys as he hit the floor.

What had they done to her?

The *carabiniere* hadn't let him see the body. All they wanted to know was why she'd left that voice message on his phone the night before. He was the last person Maria Gatti had tried to contact.

'What was she trying to tell you?' the lady copper had asked him.

'I wish I knew,' was all that he had been able to say.

The day had started badly, Simone and Ettore waiting on the doorstep when he drove into the factory car park. Simone wanted him to go to town to sign some papers. Then his mobile had rung, he'd had to answer it, and they had heard every word.

The *carabinieri* needed to speak to him immediately in Cerreto.

'No problem,' Ettore had said. 'We'll take you up there, then go to town later.'

Like guard dogs, watching over him.

They'd known what was up. It was *them* that had done it. Ettore probably. Not that it made much difference. Whatever Ettore did, Simone would have told him to do. They had loaded him into the car and told him what to say to the *carabinieri* before they dropped him off near Maria's house.

'We're customers, Antò, old friends. We'll be waiting outside.'

'Keeping an eye out for you,' Ettore added.

Maria had had an accident. That's what he'd been thinking. The *carabinieri* wouldn't let him into the house. Then the woman copper had told him what had happened the night before. Maria had been murdered. It had hit him like a bullet in the brain.

Ettore had done it.

Looking over the shoulders of the *carabinieri*, he could see Ettore and Simone standing by the Mercedes, watching what was going on.

He should have told the coppers there and then that Ettore had left the restaurant early the night before. He should have shopped the bastard. It was the perfect moment. They were there, the *carabinieri* were there, and he'd have been pointing the finger, making the accusations.

They used me, tricked me – killed my only friend, and probably that ranger too.

But the cops had sent for him, not them. *He* was the one that they suspected. He had dithered too long, telling them about the phone message, about Maria and how long they'd known each other. Then the other thing had come back to haunt him – the séance in his office, the vision that Maria had seen.

He couldn't tell them about the torso Maria had conjured up.

He couldn't tell them about that without getting himself in the shit. He was being crushed, caught between the past and the present, the coppers asking questions about the bodies sprouting like truffles all over the place, his partners killing anyone who got in their way.

Maria had seen this coming.

All except the last bit, obviously.

Or had she seen her own death in the tarot cards? Was that what she had wanted to tell him?

The *carabinieri* had asked him how he knew Maria, the male cop stifling a grin at the notion of a grown man going to a woman to have his future told with playing cards.

As the cops dismissed him, he'd been tempted again to tell them everything.

The three of them eating barbecued pork chops at the Girarrosto the night before, him telling Simone and Ettore about Maria, the tarot cards, the future looking grim. Trying to frighten them into letting him go. Trying to make them think twice. People like them, people from the south of Italy, they believed in magic, the Evil Eye, messages from Beyond the Veil.

They'd laughed at him, told him to grow up.

Then Ettore had turned the Evil Eye on him. 'You still haven't learnt, have you? You've been telling her our fucking business.'

Simone Candelora had dropped his pork chop, pinched Marra's shirt sleeve between his thumb and forefinger, wiping off the grease and the fat, smiling all the time. 'What's it all about, Antò? Last time it was the dead fucking sheep. What's the problem now?'

'That dead ranger,' he had tried to explain, 'his body found near my land. Them other bits of bone when those sheep got massacred. Then, Maria and the tarot cards. I . . . well, I thought it might be bad for business.'

'You think too much,' Ettore had said.

Then the waitress came and Simone had ordered coffee and brandy nightcaps.

Ettore didn't fancy anything. 'I'm heading back to make some phone calls.'

'Take the Merc,' Simone had said. 'Antonio here'll give me a lift.'

He and Simone had left the restaurant an hour later, around ten o'clock.

Now, he knew where Ettore had gone.

'You're a pair of animals,' he said, his mouth clogged up with blood.

He tried to spit, but before it hit the water, Ettore was on him, grabbing him by the collar, pushing his throat down hard against the porcelain, cutting off his breath.

'That mouth'll be the end of you,' Ettore snarled into his ear.

'You two are finished. Kill me, and—'

Ettore pushed his head deep into the bowl and flushed the toilet.

Water filled his nose and throat, burning into his lungs. He'd paid top-notch for one of them two-speed flushes, and Ettore had hit both buttons together. The water kept on coming, and his head was blocking the exit pipe.

Next thing, he was jerked up by the hair, gasping for breath.

'That fucking witch!' Ettore cursed. 'Now, listen to *us*, you stupid fucker. We'll tell you what to do, OK? *You – understand – me?*'

His head hit the toilet bowl three times to emphasize each word.

Then, he blanked out.

They weren't talking about him any longer.

They were still standing over him, him bleeding on the bathroom floor.

Ettore sounded tense. 'D'you think he spotted me, Simò?'

'Nah. It was over in a flash. He was too busy keeping that dinky car of his on the road. A Fiat 500? Do those things still exist?'

Marra swallowed hard, trying not to move, trying not to attract their attention.

'That lizard,' Simone Candelora was saying. 'It's so fucking obvious, Ettò. You ought to get rid of it.'

'All of us had one,' Ettore said. 'First blood, you got the lizard—'

'You had the chance to do Cangio at Soverato, and you let him get away.'

'The fucking Bersa jammed—'

'So, what do we do about this one?'

The question resounded with a kick in Marra's ribs.

Simone dropped down on his heels, stared into Antonio Marra's eye.

'You stay here this morning, feeling sick, OK, Antò? If the cops come round, you let Rosanna handle them. No visitors.'

Ettore's shoe dug sharply into the small of his back, as Simone stood up.

'I need to pee,' Ettore announced.

Marra heard the swish of a zip. Then the swish of another one. 'Me, too,' Simone Candelora said.

Two powerful jets, warm and stinking, streamed down on his head and shoulders. His face was running with urine. It was running with something else, too.

Tears.

'I wouldn't want to be seen in that state, would you, Ettò?'

'Me, neither. He looks as though he's pissed himself.'

As the pissing stopped, the tears flowed faster.

He would have given the Porsche for a clean shirt and dry trousers.

THIRTY

Lucia Grossi closed the file she was reading and looked up at him.

She wasn't wearing lipstick or her cap; her hair was tied up in a tight bun.

Cangio wondered how to read the signs. One sign was obvious, though. She was sitting behind the desk, while Jerry Esposito perched on a chair at her side. He waved Cangio towards the only other chair in the room.

The hot seat, Cangio told himself.

'What's all this about?' he asked as Jerry Esposito switched on the voice recorder.

Grossi took the lead. 'A couple of things need clearing up, Cangio. In the initial statement you made to us in Spoleto, you suggested that Marzio Diamante was concerned about black magic and satanic rituals in the national park.'

'I've already told you—'

'Tell us again,' Esposito said.

He told them again about the desecrated church in Poggiodomo, trying to say neither more nor less than he had said the last time.

'You didn't tell us what you found there,' Lucia Grossi said.

'Signs of a fire. Maybe someone had been sleeping there.'

'Black magic, signs of Satan?'

'I doubt it.'

Lucia Grossi opened the file again and glanced at the contents.

'Marzio Diamante was of a different opinion,' she said. 'How else would you explain the fact that he was asking people whether they had seen anything odd in the woods at night?'

Cangio felt his blood go cold.

Did they know about the ancient file in the bottom drawer of Marzio's filing cabinet?

Had Marzio submitted a copy of the report to his superiors?

'It's news to me,' he said. 'When was this? Recently?'

'The day before he died,' she said.

That took Cangio by surprise. 'Who did he ask?'

Lucia Grossi picked up her notepad, flicked a couple of pages. 'During our investigation we spoke to a man named Andrea Bottini. He runs a mink farm not far from Vallo di Nera. Do you know him?'

Cangio shook his head. 'Never heard of him.'

'Marzio warned him to stay out of the woods.'

'I don't see where this is going,' Cangio said. 'I don't know the man.'

'Listen carefully to me, ranger Cangio,' she said, pointing a finger at him. 'Your partner was murdered in the woods at night, yet he told Andrea Bottini to *avoid* the woods at night. You prefer the night shift, you say. Did Marzio ever warn *you* not to go out after dark?'

'No,' Cangio admitted, 'he never said a thing to me.'

Grossi and her partner exchanged a look that brought a smile to Esposito's face.

Cangio could smell a trap, but he couldn't see it. When wolves smell traps, they turn and run. But what was he supposed to do, leap out of the window?

'And then there's Maria Gatti,' Jerry Esposito piped up.

'I don't follow you,' Cangio said.

'The MO says it all,' Esposito said. 'Black magic, ritual sacrifice. It's got everything that Marzio Diamante was talking about.'

'Everyone knew she was a medium,' Cangio said.

He let it hang in the air, waiting for a reaction.

The two *carabinieri* didn't react.

They sat there, staring at him, waiting for him to go on.

'Including Antonio Marra.'

That was the moment to ask them what Marra had been doing in a car with the man with the lizard tattoo. To insist that the Calabrian mafia were tied up somehow in Marzio's murder. They could only kick him out, or accuse him of wasting their time.

'Did Marra go to Maria Gatti's house last night? Did either of his clients? Maybe you should ask them what they did after dinner,' Cangio went on.

Lucia Grossi waved her hand dismissively. 'We believe Marzio Diamante was spreading those stories for a specific purpose: frightening people away from the forest at night.'

'Why would he do that?'

'He was hiding something.'

'Like what, for example?'

'Like this, for example.'

She laid a sheet of paper on the desk and pushed it towards him, holding onto it with her fingertips while he read it, as if she didn't want to let it get away. It was the forensic report Cristina di Marco had written about the human jaw among the bones of the massacred sheep. The pathologist confirmed what she had already told him: the jaw was Asiatic, male, most probably Chinese.

'That jaw had been there quite some time,' Lucia Grossi said. She placed her elbows on her desk, formed a platform with her hands, and rested her chin on it. 'So let me ask you this, ranger Cangio. Can you tell me why a Chinese man was hacked to pieces in the national park two or three years ago?'

Cangio shifted in his seat.

Now was the time to tell her about the Chinese cigarette ends the Pastore brothers had shown him. But would he be making things any easier for himself? The evidence of his reticence was piling up. He hadn't told them about Marzio's hidden file. He couldn't tell them he had spoken with their pathologist without damaging Cristina di Marco's career. Nor had he told them about the Chinese ideogram pointing to a restaurant in Soho, London. There was probably more, but he was certainly facing a charge of compromising an official investigation into at least one murder.

'Why ask me?' he said. 'I wasn't here two or three years ago.'

Lucia Grossi's lips creased, but she wasn't smiling. 'Marzio Diamante was,' she said. 'Which raises another question. Was this Chinese man alone, or were there others? And how many other Chinese men might have crossed the national park at night more recently?'

Grossi clasped her fists on the desk in front of her.

The brightest lipstick in the world could not have softened the look on her face.

'Illegal immigrants,' she said forcefully. 'Foreigners travelling under cover of night through forests, and over mountains. We know that Chinese immigrants often land on the Adriatic coast en route to places like Prato in Tuscany, where they're sure to find work. They need an expert guide to show them the way. Someone who knows the area like the back of his hand. A park ranger, for instance.'

'A ranger who warns people to avoid the forest at night,' Esposito added. 'Marzio Diamante.'

'And whoever was helping him.'

They both stared long and hard at him.

'You can go,' Lucia Grossi said at last, 'but don't leave Umbria. It's up to the investigating magistrate to decide what happens next.'

Esposito held out his hand.

'Your identity card, please,' he said. 'Do you have a passport?'

'Not here,' Cangio lied, as he pulled his ID from his wallet.

'Leave your passport with Sustrico in Spoleto,' Lucia Grossi said. 'I'll tell him to expect you by tomorrow morning at the very latest.'

Then they let him off the hook.

For the moment.

THIRTY-ONE

ow much time did he have left?

If Grossi and Esposito had already requested a mandate, they would probably arrest him within twenty-four hours on suspicion of murdering Marzio, and maybe even Maria Gatti, too. But if they still had to convince the magistrate that they had sufficient evidence to justify arrest in either case, he might be free for a day or two at the most.

It wasn't a lot.

The problem was what to do with the time at his disposal.

He'd been mulling it over as he extricated himself from the maze of Perugia's one-way system and headed for the ring road which would take him south towards Foligno, Spoleto and Valnerina. The traffic was heavy, cars and trucks whizzing by as if they were all being hounded by the RCS. He waited for a gap in the traffic, then managed to slot himself in behind an ancient rust-eaten Fiat Panda. No one was chasing this driver, that was for sure. He might have been the only innocent soul on the road that day, he was going so slowly, and there was just no way of overtaking him.

What was the point of killing Marzio or Maria Gatti?

It all seemed to revolve around Antonio Marra, starting with the 'sightings' that Marzio had begun to document two years before. The jaw of the dead Chinese man had been found more recently near Marra's truffle reserve, but the unknown man had been hacked to death in the same time period, if the carbon-14 test on his teeth could be relied on. Then Marzio had been executed just a stone's throw away from Marra's land. And Marla Gatti was reading the cards for Marra.

There *had* to be a link.

And what about the two Calabrians? How did they fit into it? They hadn't even been in Umbria two years earlier, so far as Cangio knew. The one with the lizard tattoo certainly hadn't. If he was right, the man with the tattoo had been battering a rival Mafioso to death on Soverato beach in Calabria the summer before last.

'What now, Sebastiano?' he said out loud to himself.

As he trailed the Panda into a kilometre-and-a-half-long tunnel, hemmed in by cars in the fast lane, he wondered what to do for the best. He could drive home to Valnerina, then wait and see what happened next. Or he could take to the woods and hide out until . . .

Until what?

Unless he took the initiative, nothing was going to change. He might appeal for help, but who could he appeal to? If he voiced his suspicions to the park authorities, they'd write him off as a madman. Like Grossi and Esposito, they'd think that he was seeking attention.

Which left the *carabinieri* in Spoleto.

He had put his trust in the *carabinieri* once before. General Corsini, the ambitious head of *Carabinieri* Special Ops. He had stuck his head in the lion's mouth, and the lion had nearly bitten it off. Corsini would have left him to die, or shot him without a second's thought.

Sustrico might be a safer bet.

But then he thought of the brigadier's office, the religious icons on the walls and desk. Saying prayers together to Padre Pio or Our Lady of Lourdes wouldn't get him far. And there was Sustrico himself to take into account. Would he welcome anyone bringing him trouble? Rather than take the risk, Sustrico would pick up the phone and call the RCS. He might even decide to arrest Cangio on the spot and show those two high-flyers in Perugia what a hot-shot cop he was.

There was a gap in the fast lane.

He hit the indicator and swung to the left.

'*Ciao, amore!*' he said, as the Panda disappeared from view.

And that was when lightning struck. A publicity poster flashed into view for an instant. A bright yellow sign with angular black symbols, the town of Assisi and the basilica of Saint Francis providing a backdrop on the hill behind it. It was almost as if Saint Francis was telling him what to do, and where to go.

When the sign to Foligno appeared ten minutes later, he took the exit.

'Why would they be crossing the mountains?'

Cangio was in the Chinese restaurant, the Szechuan, in the centre of Foligno, talking to Heng Lu, the restaurant owner, who looked at him through narrowed, perplexed eyes.

It was late afternoon and the restaurant was empty. Cangio didn't want to eat, in any case. He wanted to ask Heng Lu some questions, and the Chinese gave him a beer to humour him.

Cangio was a customer, after all.

'The police believe that illegal immigrants land on the east coast, then they cross the mountains on foot heading for Tuscany. Most Chinese people end up working as slaves in the clandestine sweatshops of Prato, apparently.'

'That's true, but it doesn't make sense,' Heng Lu protested. 'These people . . .' He rubbed his forefinger against his nose, and Cangio noticed that half the finger was missing. 'The Triad doesn't mess about. Walk across the mountains? Ha! They'd take them in a van with a padlock on the door!'

'What if they were walking the other way, towards the Adriatic coast?'

'What would they be going out there for? The coast is dead in winter. There's no work, no Chinese community.'

They were sitting next to the kitchen in the empty restaurant far away from the picture window looking out onto the street. A young Chinese man in a grubby T-shirt was laying the tables. Each time he pushed through the swing door, Cangio saw a battery of pans on the stove giving off lots of steam, which smelled of boiling fish. The young man didn't look at Cangio or his boss; in fact, he made no acknowledgement that they were there as he put his shoulder to the swing door and went back into the kitchen again.

'Where did he come from?' Cangio asked, glancing towards the kitchen.

Heng Lu stared at him, then glanced to the front door of the restaurant again, as if he really did fear that someone might be spying on him.

Cangio wondered just how complicated Heng Lu's life was. He had spoken of the Triad. Was someone keeping a watchful eye on him and his restaurant? One of those violent gangs the Chinese were renowned for, people who might actually be involved in the trafficking of human beings?

'Xin's my nephew. He's been here five years now. Xin travelled by lorry to Albania, then he took a ride in a rubber boat one night.'

'By lorry? From China to Albania?'

'That's one of the routes. One of the cheapest.'

Xin came over, bowed to his uncle and said something in Chinese.

Heng Lu nodded, watching the boy as he headed for the door. 'He's taking a five-minute break for a smoke before the evening rush begins. But now let us talk about *your* smokers. Those Chinese cigarettes . . . If you ask me, they came here by plane. Lots of tourists fly from Stansted to Perugia. I've been to London myself on holiday. They probably went back the same way.'

'*If* they went back—'

'Tourists always go back.'

Cangio could have corrected him on that score, but he didn't. 'So what do you think they were doing in the Sibillines National Park?'

Heng Lu stuck out his jaw, his mouth clamped tight. 'What do people usually do there?' His puzzlement seemed genuine. He was only twenty-five kilometres away, but he swore that he had never been to the national park, or gone to see the rivers and mountains.

'They walk, climb, go rafting, watch birds and wild animals . . .'

'Are Chinese tourists any different?'

Cangio hesitated before replying.

'Some human remains were found in the park last week,' he said.

'I read about it in *Corriere dell'Umbria*.'

'What you didn't read was the fact that the bones belonged to a Chinese man. This man was hacked to bits, and the remains of his body were buried in the park. The question is what was he doing there?'

Heng Lu took a pack of cigarettes from the pocket of his shirt. He put one in his mouth, but he didn't light it. The cigarettes were MS Lite, a popular Italian brand, Cangio noted.

'Have you heard of any Chinese person disappearing in the last few years?' he asked. 'A person who was living in Foligno, or in Umbria?'

'If he'd belonged to my community, I would have heard about it.'

Cangio pulled a face. 'Would you have told the police?'

Heng Lu laughed, and then lit his cigarette. 'We keep our secrets to ourselves,' he said. 'Let's stick to what we know. Those cigarettes came from London. Whoever smoked them came from there, or had been to London recently. I told you the name of the restaurant in Soho, remember?'

'Butterfly,' Cangio said, as if it were a test.

'That's where I'd start looking. London.'

Heng Lu sniffed the air. 'Do you want to try the steamed sea bass with ginger? It's ready, if you ask me.'

Cangio jumped to his feet. 'Next time, maybe.'

'Bring your girlfriend,' Heng Lu said.

'Maybe,' Cangio said.

If we're still together, he thought.

THIRTY-TWO

Cangio drove out of Foligno.

What would a wolf do with the hunters closing in?

The wolf would find a way of distancing itself from the danger. There was only one escape path open, so far as he could see. If he went back home, he'd be heading for trouble.

As he reached the super highway which would take him south,

he spotted a road sign, a distinctive white symbol on a blue enamel background. As he joined the queue of lorries going onto the slip road, he saw the blue-and-white sign again, an arrow pointing north.

On an impulse he flashed his indicator, then followed the sign. It took him twenty minutes to get there.

The airport was new – relatively new, at any rate – and carefully laid out with a wide approach road and large billboards that proudly announced that the airport had been refurbished in 2011 with a mountain of money from a special fund set up to celebrate the one hundred and fiftieth anniversary of the Unity of Italy. Now, it was known officially as the Saint Francis of Assisi airport. In a brighter mood, he might have laughed. The saint had preached to the birds of the air, but he would have needed to shout loud if he wanted to preach to the jets.

The car park was huge, far larger than necessary, given the few cars that were parked there. He pulled up in front of the Arrivals building, got out, then locked the door, though it was hard to imagine any airport thief choosing a humble Fiat 500 over one of the gleaming SUVS, BMWs, Mercedes and smaller utility vehicles that seemed to make up the sum of cars belonging to passengers who were overseas, blissfully uncertain of whether their wheels would still be there when they got back from their holidays or business trips.

The Arrivals building was vast and empty, except for a couple of paunchy middle-aged men in uniform, who were standing by the check-in counter chatting to a couple of pretty girls in dark blue uniforms and caps. The information desk in the far corner was unmanned. The airport of St Francis of Assisi looked as dead as the proverbial duck.

He checked the arrivals board: Bucharest, the Greek island of Rhodes, Timişoara in Rumania, Brindisi, London. All the flights had landed before five p.m., and it was now half-past six.

As he walked in the direction of the hostesses, the men in uniform exchanged a 'here-comes-a-balls-breaker' glance.

'Excuse me,' he asked. 'Are there any more flights coming in?'

'Finished for the day,' one of the girls said, though her gaze lingered. Cangio was twenty-nine years old, dark-haired, brown-eyed, tanned and fit – younger, slimmer and taller than either of the watching men. 'Were you expecting someone?' she said, pulling away from the group. 'If we step across to the main information desk, I can check today's passenger lists for you.'

She beamed a warm smile at him, then turned and strode away, showing off a fine figure and a nice pair of legs, her medium-high heels clicking on the marble floor, echoing around the empty building.

Cangio followed, of course.

Not just the girl, but the impulse that had brought him to the airport.

'Now,' she said, tapping a keyboard and glancing at a computer screen. 'Have you lost somebody? A passenger? You'd be surprised how often it happens.'

'It was more of a general enquiry,' he improvised. 'I'm a ranger in the Sibillines National Park. We . . . that is, I . . .'

She looked at him and cocked her head. 'Really? I've never met a ranger before.'

Cangio smiled back at her. 'I was wondering whether we might be able to attract more visitors to the park by advertising here in the airport,' he said.

'That *is* a good idea,' she said with emphasis. 'We're a fully fledged international airport these days. Well, sort of. We have passengers coming in from London every day. Ryanair keeps us pretty busy. There are flights to Germany, Spain and . . . oh, yes, Greece, a couple of times a week.' She leant forward, and lowered her voice. 'We have quite a lot of flights to Eastern Europe – Rumania, Bulgaria, Ukraine. Those are charter flights for the most part, migrant workers coming and going . . .'

'What about Japan, the Far East?' he asked. 'Many of our park visitors seem to come from those places.'

She shook her head and made a tutting noise. 'That would be the cherry on the cake,' she said. 'The Japanese are the biggest spenders, but they fly in and out of Rome or Milan, not some small provincial watering hole like this one.'

'So a Chinese passenger, let's say, would be a rarity?'

'Oh, no,' she said. 'Quite a few fly in with Ryanair from London.'

'That's just what I was hoping you would say.'

She flashed him a bright smile. 'What's your name?'

'Seb,' he said. 'Sebastiano.'

'Like the saint who got himself shot full of arrows?' she joked. 'Listen, Seb, buy me a coffee, save me from those two slobs over there, and I'll tell you everything you want to know about the passengers who fly in to Assisi.'

THIRTY-THREE

Ettore's mobile phone rang.

He was feeling good. They'd shared a couple of lines up in Simone's room. Top-rate stuff, his head was buzzing, his nose itching for more. Now they were in the hotel bar drinking Aperol in front of the big picture window. Outside the arc lights were on, showing off the Roman bridge and the spectacular view.

'Yeah?' said Ettore, and listened carefully for a couple of minutes.

When he ended the call he turned to Simone. 'That ranger, Cangio.'

'What about him?'

'He was at the airport asking questions. Our customs man spotted him as he was going on duty, said he'd seen the ranger on the telly when he got shot.'

'What was he doing there? Asking about us?'

'Nah,' Ettore said. 'He was chatting up the hostesses, asking about foreign tourists, talking about the park, apparently.'

'So, what's the problem?' Simone said. 'He's just doing his job. You've got a thing about him, you have.'

'*Thing*?' Ettore sat up fast.

Drops of Aperol spattered his white shirt like fresh blood.

'I should have blown him away in Soverato.'

'You'll get another chance,' Simone said.

Cangio didn't go home that night.

First, he switched off his mobile phone. Then he phoned Lori from a payphone at the airport and told her that his own phone was being repaired.

'Are you OK?' she said, and she sounded worried.

He put a lot of effort into saying, 'Fine, just fine.'

They chatted for a couple of minutes, then he said, 'I'll be off the air for a couple of days,' then he blew her a kiss and said goodbye.

OK, he thought, he had a ski jacket in the car. He had money in his wallet, a credit card with a healthy balance. Most important of all, he had his passport in his breast pocket. He always carried it around with him. Ever since leaving Soverato. You never knew when you were going to need it. And those two clots from the RCS had taken him at his word, telling him to take it to Sustrico in Spoleto the following day instead.

He climbed into the Fiat 500 and considered his next move.

He stopped off in a service station on the SS75, ate dinner there, then drove to a rest area a few kilometres away and slept in his vehicle like the half-dozen lorry drivers from Croatia, France and Austria who chose to pass the night in their artics rather than spend their allowance on a hotel.

The only problem was the Fiat 500.

It was so small, you couldn't stretch out, couldn't get comfortable.

Then again, the fact that the car was so small had one advantage. None of the tarts working the parking lot bothered to knock on his window that night. Turning tricks was one thing. But in a Fiat 500?

Ettore was shaving next morning when his mobile phone rang.

He glanced at his watch. It was way too early for anyone, even Candelora.

'Yeah?'

He listened for a bit without saying a word, then said, 'What time?'

Then he phoned Simone Candelora and told him what he had in mind.

THIRTY-FOUR

The plane was three-quarters full.

Most of the passengers looked like OAPs, while the rest of them were teachers and teenagers going on a school trip, maybe to see the Queen, Ettore thought.

He was sitting at the tail end of the aircraft, keeping an eye on everything, wearing a scarf to hide the lizard tattoo, a tan-coloured raincoat over that because it always rained in England, they said.

That was all he knew about London.

He had never been there, and wouldn't have been going today, except for the fact that the ranger was on the plane.

Sebastiano Cangio was sitting near the front.

Ettore wondered what the ranger was up to. It hardly seemed like a time to go on holiday, his partner's head blown off, and the police investigation in full swing, hotting up probably, on account of the corpse that had turned up in Cerreto two days before – that witch, Maria Gatti, or whatever her name was.

What had the cops made of that, he asked himself. According to the newspaper, the *carabinieri* were taking the spooky side of it seriously. And why not, Ettore thought, two dead, headless bodies in the national park in the space of ten days? Lopping off the medium's head and planting that bread knife in her heart had been an act of genius.

As the plane began to roll along the runway, Ettore gripped the seat and felt his stomach roll. The don would be pleased when Cangio was no longer around to trouble them. A third killing in the park, though, there would have been no end to it. The papers were already talking about a serial killer. But if Cangio were to simply disappear, they might decide he had run away because he'd done it . . .

Was he doing the right thing?

Going back to London had not been something he'd been planning on.

Cangio remembered how relieved he'd been to get away from the city, the lousy job with the estate agency, the sense of alienation he had felt so far away from his friends, his home and Italy.

Away from the wolves of the Apennine mountains.

He had felt reborn in the national park, but then the 'Ndrangheta had come along and shattered the dream.

But you couldn't run away and hide.

He had tried in London, and it hadn't worked. He had tried again in Umbria, and had nearly lost his life to an 'Ndrangheta bullet. And now the mob was back in Valnerina, and the key to the puzzle seemed to lie in London's Chinese quarter.

If he could find out what connected a Chinese jaw, some cigarette ends from a Soho restaurant, and the truffle reserve of Antonio Marra, he might be able to convince Lucia Grossi and Jerry Esposito to point the accusing finger somewhere else. He owed it to Marzio.

And to himself, of course.

He gripped the arms of the seat as the plane lifted off with a sudden upward lurch.

If there was one thing he hated more than London, it was flying.

THIRTY-FIVE

London.

Was he seeing things?

Cangio stared at the small glass jars on the shelf. He might have put it down to jet lag, changing time zones, the constant thrum of engines, but the flight from Assisi had barely lasted two hours, and the plane had touched down with a fanfare of trumpets and minutes to spare. Just five and a half hours after leaving Italy, he had been walking down Gerrard Street, looking for a sign, and he had found it without any trouble.

Next door to a large supermarket was the biggest restaurant

on the block, and both premises sported the same bright ideogram, a word spelled out in English for tourists who didn't speak Chinese: *Butterfly*.

Butterfly was the major supplier of Chinese merchandise in London, according to Heng Lu, the owner of the Chinese restaurant in Foligno. The cigarette ends the Pastore brothers had found had come from there. But he needed to come up with something fast, or he would really be in trouble. Once Grossi and Esposito got wind of where he was, they would accuse him of murder and put out an international warrant for his arrest.

For an instant, it crossed his mind to stay in London and never go back.

He had enough money to survive for a few weeks, he had his passport, and it wouldn't be difficult to find a job of some sort. He had hidden out in London once before, and he could do it again. Maybe he'd been a fool to go back to Italy the last time.

There was only one thing he was sure of: an 'Ndrangheta bullet would be waiting for him in Umbria if the cops didn't catch him first.

The restaurant wasn't open, so he went into the supermarket.

A man behind the cash desk glanced his way as he walked through the door, muttered something that might have been a greeting, then turned back to the Chinese video he was watching on a large flat screen fixed to the wall.

It was a bit like walking into an Aladdin's cave of exotic foods.

He walked up and down the aisles, stopping now and then to read the contents of the brightly coloured boxes, tins and packets on display. He was amazed by the variety of the genuine Chinese goods on offer, including a mysterious concoction labelled *Bright Red Powder*.

Inspired by Mao, he wondered.

The shelves went on and on. Shrimp paste, fish paste, lobster paste, crab broth cubes. Bottles and tubes galore. Packets of sweets and biscuits, the ingredients printed out in Chinese characters. It took him ten minutes to work his way around the supermarket, but it was only when he got to the final aisle that his heart skipped a beat.

A shelf was packed with small glass jars, rows and rows of them, different brands and different names: *Tuber indicium*, *Tuber himalayensis, Tuber sinensis.* A placard marked *Szechuan truffles* showed a photo of the area where the tubers were grown. If not for the bent backs, wide straw hats and half-mast trousers of the labourers planting them, it might have been the valley of the River Nera where he was living in Italy. Szechuan was in the foothills of the Himalayan mountains, the placard said. Cold in winter, hot in summer, rain in spring and autumn (the planting seasons), endless woods and chalky soil.

Just like Umbria, but eight thousand kilometres away.

Ettore covered the mouthpiece with his hand.

The place was swarming with tipsy tourists taking pictures.

'I'm in a street full of dragons,' he said. 'There's this big wooden gate, and the place is steaming with Chinkies. Even the fucking bugs have got slit eyes. I thought this was London, Simò . . .'

He looked the other way as a group of noisy Italian tourists wafted by.

'You're in Chinatown,' Simone Candelora told him.

Ettore glanced around, looking for a printed sign that might resemble the sound that Simone the Smart-arse had made. He hated it when someone played the know-all at his expense. Blood had been spilled, lives lost when someone took the piss out of him.

'That's where he dragged me,' Ettore spat back.

The flight had been a nightmare. Bumps and jolts from start to finish. He hated flying, all closed up in a long tube with a toilet tighter than a coffin, heading for disaster. He'd had to use the toilet twice: once to throw up, the other time to ease the cramp in his guts, caused by the growing panic as the flight stretched out. He'd started feeling better when they landed. Now, the vile cooking smells and the stringy roasted ducks hanging up in the restaurant windows were making him feel sick again.

Still, he had Cangio boxed up inside the supermarket.

The ranger had been easy to follow; first a train, then a taxi.

Cangio had flown to London, then 'disappeared without a trace'. That was how the papers in Italy would spell it out. That was how Don Michele would hear it. He wouldn't bother asking who had done them all a favour.

'He's in a Chinese shop,' Ettore said.

'Has he spotted you?'

'Nah. He's too friggin' busy.'

'So what he doing in there?'

Ettore didn't have an answer. He couldn't figure out why Cangio was in London, though the ranger seemed to know what he was up to, moving about from place to place like a man with a purpose.

'How the fuck should I know?'

Ettore kept his eyes on the supermarket windows, watching Cangio wander up and down the aisles, fingering stuff here and there, reading labels, buying nothing.

There was no way of knowing what was going on in his head.

'He's been in there fifteen minutes,' Ettore reported.

'*Jesus Maria santa!* You wanted to follow him to London? Fucking follow him, then! Find out what he's up to, then call me back. This isn't a tourist jaunt, remember!'

The phone went dead in Ettore's hand.

'What d'you think I'm doing?' he said, and cursed the phone as if it were the face of Simone Candelora himself.

Cangio was on the other side of the plate glass window.

The ranger hadn't moved an inch. He was holding something in his hand, staring out of the window, talking into his own mobile phone. Not staring at *him*, mind, just staring like he was concentrating, listening hard, or something.

'Who the fuck are you calling?' Ettore hissed through his teeth.

The voice came over loud and clear.

It might have been coming from the other side of the street, the signal was so strong.

'It'd be like an alien invasion, Cangio. Worse! They're . . . what do you call it, camouflaged? They look right, feel right, but they ain't right. They ain't right at *all*. They're aliens, like I told you. OK, they *look* like ours, but they're a load of rubbish. They're stronger than ours, though, more ferocious. If they get a hold, and that's what they'll do, they'll wipe us out in less than no time!'

Manlio Pastore might have been talking about *War of the Worlds*.

'Manlio, have you been watching sci-fi films?'

'I'm talking about the *Tuber indicium*,' Manlio Pastore snapped. 'Those are monsters you've got locked up in that jar.'

'They look just like the ones that you find. A black blob in a small glass jar. Same size, same shape . . .'

Manlio snorted. 'They're poison, they are. Big, black poisonous spiders! They multiply like horseflies. Plant twenty of them in Umbria, and you'd wipe out the whole autochthonous population.'

Autochthonous?

Cangio began to take the man seriously.

'Every local truffle would die,' Manlio ranted on. 'Not die, but change. That's the danger. Once the spores start to spread, once the fungivores get started, the foxes, squirrels and wild boar start carrying the disease around on their fur, that would be it. Our truffles would lose their taste and perfume. It would be the end, I tell you.'

Cangio turned the jar in his fingers, examining it the way a gem merchant might have studied a diamond to see if it was real or synthetic.

'They look as good as anything you'll find in Umbria.'

'Leave them fucking things where they are!' Manlio shouted. 'I'm warning you, Cangio. If you come back to Italy with those, I'll have you locked up good, I will. There's a law, you know, decree 752, 1985, article 18. Do you hear me? Oi, Cangio, can you hear—'

Cangio pressed the button and cut off the voice.

The line began to buzz as though it was an insect closed inside the small glass jar he was holding in his other hand.

THIRTY-SIX

The street was like a river in flood.

A fat woman marched past like a sergeant major, holding up a flag of parallel red-and-yellow stripes. Her group came trundling after her. They were Spaniards, by the sound of them. They kept on saying *mucho, mucho*. Oh yeah, and *gracias*, too, swarming all around him like a rock that wouldn't shift.

Ettore took a breath and waded into the stream, a man with a mission, pushing his way across to the other bank, ignoring the complaints, taking a tap or two on the ankles, pressing on until he got there. He wasn't going to lose the ranger because of a bunch of lousy Spanish gits.

He emerged from the ruck, and Cangio had disappeared.

'Where are you?' he cursed. 'Where the fuck?'

Cangio backtracked through the aisles.

He was looking for a girl he'd seen stocking shelves.

He found her working in the noodles section, putting out plastic packs of something called Cat's Ears.

'I'd like to speak to the manager,' he said.

The girl was wearing a black nylon uniform with a bright yellow Butterfly symbol on the collar. Lank and pale-faced, her black her cut short, she could have been twelve years old. She closed her eyes, shook her head at him, and said, 'No English.'

He tried again, miming someone big, fat and important. 'The boss?'

She cocked her head, then pointed back towards the entrance door. He recalled his reception as he had walked into the supermarket. The man behind the check-out watching a Chinese video.

Ettore was frantic.

He bustled into the supermarket, looked down all of the aisles.

Cangio had disappeared. If he hadn't come out, he could only be in there somewhere.

Maybe he'd gone to the toilet, or something?

In the last aisle, he checked the shelf that Cangio had been interested in, and let out a whistle. He left the shop, retreated to a doorway on the other side of the street. He'd smoke a cigarette, see what happened. He couldn't wait to tell Candelora what that piece of shit had been doing in the shop.

First, he lit his cigarette, then he pulled out his mobile.

THIRTY-SEVEN

He'd sometimes heard it said that the Chinese show no emotion.

It might be true in China, but it wasn't true in the West.

Not always, Cangio thought.

Still, Heng Lu, the Chinese man from Foligno, was an open book compared to the stone-faced man behind the supermarket check-out. He listened, nodded, hissed a few sibilant words in Chinese into a phone, and then pointed Cangio to a bare wooden staircase. All without a single word in English.

At the top of the stairs was a door.

He knocked and a voice said, 'Come in.'

A tiny Chinese man was sitting behind a large black lacquered desk.

There was nothing big, or fat, or important-looking about him.

There was nothing on his desk, except for a big red button and a black plastic telephone that must have been fifty years old. A battery of six TV monitors was mounted on the wall in front of him.

'Can I help you?' the man asked.

'I'm looking for Mister . . . Butterfly,' Cangio said.

The little man smiled, showing large front teeth. 'Mister Butterfly?' he said. 'I like that. You got lucky, mister. I am Mister Butterfly.'

He let out a chuckle, then pressed the red button.

'Don't worry,' he said as Cangio baulked. 'It's no atomic bomb. In my business, we look after the customers very good. My name is Li Liü Gong, though maybe, yes, Mister Butterfly is easier.'

He seemed to like the idea.

The Chinese nodded at the monitors. 'I thought we'd get to talk,' he said. 'You spent a lot of time examining my shelves, and then you didn't buy anything.'

'I was looking at the truffles,' Cangio said, unsure how to play it. 'You've got an amazing selection on display.'

'We call them *tubers*,' the man corrected him. 'It's more scientific, less problematical, too. European laws, you know, are so protective. We favour unrestricted trade in China. We let the customer choose, as he or she has every right to do. So, now, Mister . . .'

'Cangio. Sebastiano Cangio.'

'What precisely interests you about the tubers?'

Cangio turned in his seat as the door opened, and a boy came in.

'*Mòlìhuā chá*,' he said with a bow, as he set a tray down on the desk.

'Jasmine tea,' Mister Butterfly translated, as the boy left them alone.

'That's kind of you,' Cangio said, wondering if everyone admitted to the presence of the great man immediately required a restorative cup of tea.

On the wall behind the desk was a calendar in Chinese characters showing Butterfly restaurants in Islington, Ealing, and others parts of London, plus a larger photo of the flagship Soho eating house next door to where they were sitting.

'In Italy, we have truffles,' Cangio said, '*tubers*, if you prefer, which look very similar to yours.' He gave a shrug. 'I was wondering about them. Your prices seem so very low . . . I mean to say, how do they compare in quality? Do the Chinese variety taste the same as our Italian truffles?'

Li Liü Gong poured tea for them both, then raised his cup in a sort of toast.

Cangio burnt his fingers on the cup, drinking off the contents in a single draught.

'Do you trade in truffles, Mister Cangio?'

Hearing his name on the Chinese man's tongue, he wondered whether he should have given himself a false one. It hardly mattered, did it? He was deceiving the man, whichever name he used.

'You are Italian, do I guess right?'

Cangio nodded. 'I've been thinking of expanding into import and export. Truffles would play a big part in the business, but . . .

well . . .' He was considering the impediments – limited finances, limited knowledge, fierce competition – when Li Liü Gong came up with the solution, as if he had heard the argument before.

'But you don't have enough land to produce a sufficient quantity.' He waved his hand to crush the hypothesis, as if it were laughable. 'Tubers are rare in Italy, I know, and they are very expensive. Unless you have the *right* land, and lots of it, it's never going to turn into a profitable business. Do I guess right again?'

Mister Butterfly seemed to enjoy the rhetorical question.

Cangio held up his palms in surrender. 'You guessed correctly,' he said.

'So you want me to send you Chinese tubers?'

Cangio made a face at that suggestion. 'Those European laws you mentioned before . . .'

Mister Butterfly nodded. 'I understand,' he said. 'What you really want is *know-how*. Help, let's say, to make your land produce more tubers. *Truffles*, let's call them now, because that's what you'll be exporting, isn't it?'

He poured more tea, then looked at Cangio over the rim of his teacup.

Cangio stared back at him, then nodded twice.

'You can help me, Mister Butterfly, do *I* guess right?'

The Chinese drained his cup, then set it down on the table. 'You will eat in my restaurant tonight, I hope? You'll be my guest. I'll have them prepare some special dishes for you with our tubers. Then you'll know exactly how they taste. How does that sound?'

'It sounds good.'

'Are you from Alba, Mister Cangio? The finest white truffles come from the north.'

'No,' Cangio said, 'I come from Umbria, in central Italy.'

'Umbria?' the Chinese man repeated with a frown. Apart from showing his teeth in a smile, it was the first expression Cangio had read upon his face. 'I had some . . . dealings with a man from Umbria once. A most distressing experience.' His expression reminded Cangio of someone recalling a serious illness, or a painful operation. 'I would not wish to repeat it, I can tell you. We will talk some more over dinner, Mister Cangio. I want to know more about you and your affairs. But now, I have my own business to look after. If you will excuse me?'

Which 'distressing experience' was Mister Butterfly talking of?

Had the same 'distressing experience' led to cigarette ends from the Butterfly restaurant being found in Valnerina?

Cangio went downstairs and bought himself a bottle of Szechuan truffles.

They were as cheap as baked beans.

THIRTY-EIGHT

'This'll blow you away, Simò,' Ettore said into the phone.

'What will?'

'He just walked out of a supermarket. All the way to London, and what's he doing?'

Candelora snorted. 'Cut the quiz, and get it over with.'

Simone was in a nasty mood, though you couldn't blame him, could you? The ranger skipping Italy like that, offering them the chance to knock him off without creating trouble for Don Michele in Umbria. And then the mystery that put the block on everything: they needed to know what the fuck the ranger was doing in London before they made a move.

'Find out!' Simone had told him. 'We *have* to know, Ettore.'

Just like that. *We have to know*. As if it was easy. *He* was the one in London, a place he'd never been before. All he wanted to do was pick the right moment, kill the ranger, then get back on a plane to Italy without the British cops latching on to him.

'You really want to know what this dickhead's up to?' Ettore knew he was losing his temper, but so what! 'Chinese fucking truffles. That what he's doing in London, Simò. That's what he came here for. That's what he was looking at.'

'Truffles?'

'You want me to spell it for you?'

Simone let go a string of curses.

Ettore held the phone away from his ear, only caught the last bit.

'. . . Don't lose sight of him, Ettò, you hear me? See what he does next.'

Cangio had almost forgotten how crowded London could be.

It was Friday night, beer night, club night, hen night. The streets were thronged with people out for a lark at the end of another deadly working week, plus armies of foreign tourists. Outside every pub, a horde of boozers crowded the pavement, glass in one hand, cigarette in the other, spilling out onto the street. Women in shorts and see-through blouses, high-heeled ankle-snappers. Men in suits, their silk ties dangling loose. There were long queues outside the cinemas in Leicester Square. Open-air restaurants with big, fancy sunshades had every table taken, though the night air was cold and the wind cut sharp.

It seemed like more than a year since he'd left it all behind, and he hadn't missed it once. In Umbria, he'd found what he was looking for. Everything he was looking for. And now those two, Grossi and Esposito, were threatening to take it all away, treating him and Marzio like a pair of slave-traders, more or less, suggesting they were ferrying illegal Chinese immigrants across the park at night. It made him ill just thinking about it. Unless he could prove that they were wrong, he'd probably end up going to jail for quite a few years. Which meant losing everything. His job, the park, the wolves, Loredana.

But now he had something to show them.

He had the proof in his pocket. A jar of cheap Chinese truffles.

And Mister Butterfly could tell him more.

Perplexity was growing on Ettore's brow.

Where was Cangio going? What was he up to?

They seemed to be wandering around aimlessly in a big circle.

It wasn't easy keeping him in sight among the crowds.

It meant moving closer, shortening the gap, increasing the risk of being spotted.

He was so busy watching the ranger, before he knew it, he found himself back in Chinatown outside the Chinese supermarket again.

This time, Cangio didn't go into the shop, he went into the restaurant next door.

THIRTY-NINE

Simone Candelora ordered a bottle of Franciacorta.

He was sitting in the bar of the hotel by the picture window, looking out at the Roman bridge and the limestone gorge, the scene lit up by glaring spotlights courtesy of some generous corporate sponsor.

He needed to calm down, consider the situation, think it through.

It was a beautiful view, the honey-coloured bridge silhouetted against the pitch dark woods.

If everything went the way he hoped, he'd buy the place within six months. A private investment, without telling anyone. He wouldn't run the gaff, of course. He'd leave that to the present owner, who was always on hand for a chat and a cigarette, and happy to sell the place at the first decent offer. That way, he'd have a place to stay when he was in town, a luxury five-star suite of his own with a fabulous view. He might even tell the don about it, invite him up for the weekend, show the boss what he was capable of doing on his own.

Alea iacta est.

Look, boss. I threw my dice, and this is how it landed.

But Ettore would have to go, there was no doubt about it.

He was rough, uncouth, a killer, nothing more.

No brains, no sense. A liability.

The sooner he got shut of Ettore the better. All he had to do was tell the don the fucker had outlived his usefulness, that he was more of a danger than an asset. That lizard branded on his neck was an advert for trouble, a magnet for the cops.

Ettore couldn't shoot a pigeon without the pigeon shitting on his shoes.

London would be his last outing, the end of the ride.

He could only hope the ranger hadn't recognised Ettore that

day in the car coming back from Maria Gatti's. Cangio wasn't stupid. The ranger had a brain, all right. If he guessed Ettore was on his tail, anything could happen. If Ettore had known his way around London, it would have helped, of course. Then again, Ettore's instinct might kick in. If he could lure the ranger down to the river, do the job and chuck the corpse in the Thames. The river was deep; the tides were fast. Bam, splash, and goodbye Cangio!

Did Ettore know about the river?

He sipped his Franciacorta, thought of Cangio's corpse hanging by a noose beneath Blackfriars Bridge, like that crook they called 'God's banker'. The Brits seemed to think it had been a suicide. If they bought that, they'd swallow anything. Why shift out of the hotel bathroom if you wanted to snuff yourself? Why bother climbing walls and scaling the underside of a bridge at night to do it? That investigation always made him laugh. For months, the coppers had been fucking about, and now, years later, they still had trouble seeing how it was done. With a pointed gun and a helping hand, anything was possible. That had been a classic scenario, a mystery that lingered on, a warning to the world. Don't mess with us – whoever *us* happened to be. Whoever needed to know, they knew.

Simone helped himself to a truffle canapé from the plate. He preferred caviar, of course, but if he was really honest, he had to admit that this bit of oily, dirty-looking goo was very tasty, especially with a sparkling fresh, cold wine.

A refined taste for an educated palate.

Talking of which, he wondered why Cangio was so interested in Chinese truffles all of a sudden. They were shit by all accounts. Suddenly he wondered if Ettore had got it wrong. Maybe the ranger had caught on that he was being followed and was laying traps for Ettore.

He drank more wine and sank back into the comfy old Chesterfield.

Why bust an ulcer over it? Let Ettore work it out. The sooner Ettò did the job, the sooner he could tell the don it was time to get rid of him. They'd been talking on the phone again that afternoon. Don Michele liked the way he'd handled the Maria Gatti thing, saying what a great idea it had been. The don took the credit for it, obviously, though it was Ettore who had done the actual butchering.

'Satan in Umbria,' the don had read from a newspaper. 'Great title, that.'

He had almost let slip that Ettore was in London.

Best to see how it worked out first. If it came out badly, he'd tell the don that Ettore had done it off his own bat without asking him. Everything that *he* had done in Umbria was working out nicely, thank you very much! The hub was up and running. Marra Truffles was the ideal refining plant. The airport was perfect. Once Ettore topped the ranger far away from the action in Umbria, there'd be no stopping them.

No stopping *him*, he corrected himself.

It all depended on Ettore.

Ettore smiled to himself.

Restaurants were ideal. People relaxing, taking it easy, having a drink and a meal with family or friends, glancing from one table to the next, seeing all the faces, forgetting them in an instant. No place was better than a packed Chinkie restaurant in the centre of London on a Friday night.

How many targets had he wasted in restaurants or bars?

The number five leapt instantly to mind, but he was certain there'd been a few more.

No witness had ever managed to describe him to the coppers. No one had ever mentioned the lizard tattoo, not even when he walked into a shop or supermarket wearing one of those full-face crash helmets with a shotgun in his hand. People froze, that was the truth of it. They were so shocked, so frightened of getting blasted, they would dive under the table, look the other way or not look at all.

Only Cangio had ever looked.

But not for long.

Ettore pulled the scarf from his neck and stuffed it into his pocket.

He wanted the ranger to see him, wanted him to know that this was the end.

He didn't have the sawn-off shotgun this time, so he couldn't blast the fucker the way he'd wasted that mate of his, that ranger as he came charging out of the bushes with a toy gun, saying *Stick 'em up!* OK, so no gun, but there'd be something he could use. This time, there'd be no running off to London.

They were *in* fucking London.

And this time, Cangio's seat would be empty on the plane going home.

Candelora washed down the last canapé with some wine.

There was still a little left in the bottle in the chiller bucket, another glass maybe.

There were other guests in the bar now, not many, but all classy.

His sort of people, except for the fact that most of them would be pushing up the daisies very soon. The old dear sitting at the next table, for instance, reading the newspaper. She looked as if she was getting ready to leave, picking up a big crocodile handbag that must have cost a packet thirty years ago, putting away her reading glasses. The bag was probably crammed full of gold and jewels, he imagined, the old girl carrying her worldly goods around for fear of losing them, which made her easy meat for the next lucky bag-snatcher.

He smiled as she struggled to push herself out of the low-slung chair.

The owner of the hotel appeared as if by magic, a genuine Prince Charming, offering his arm like he was planning to carry her off to a ball at the palace. A real bit of elegance, that. A proper gentleman, if you valued that sort of thing.

Simone was definitely going to keep him on as the manager.

As the old woman stood up, the newspaper she'd been reading slid to the parquet floor.

Anyone can play the gent, Simone decided, jumping up to retrieve the paper and return it to its rightful owner, show that hotel owner a thing or two.

He bent over to pick up the paper, but he didn't get up again.

The headline froze him rigid: big black letters on the page given over to Perugia.

He read the words, picked the paper up, then sat down again on the big old Chesterfield, all thoughts of comfort and gallantry flown away.

He poured the last glass from the bottle that had cost him sixty euro, threw it back, and the fizzy wine exploded like bleach in the back of his throat. The burp he let out turned every head in the lounge-bar.

It turned the head of the hotel owner, too.

He was standing in the doorway with the old girl on his arm.

Simone's attempted smile of apology was met with an icy stare.

Fuck you! Candelora thought. Your ulcer would give *you* gip as well, if you'd just read that your world was about to fall apart, and that your life was on the line.

He swallowed air, let out the loudest belch he could manage, then made for the exit.

FORTY

Candelora had been raving on the phone.

Ettore hadn't understood the half of it. OK, he was angry, but so fucking what? Something Simò had read in the paper, saying something about needing to find Antonio Marra *pronto*. Marra wasn't answering his mobile. Simone had to find the little twat and shut his mouth, he said, before it was too late.

Too late for what?

There was no stopping Simone.

The only thing that Ettore had understood was this: he had to eliminate Cangio, while Simone would take care of Antonio Marra.

'*Take care of him?*' Ettore had asked. 'What's that supposed to mean?'

Candelora went wild, spitting out a torrent of curses. 'I'm gonna wring that bastard's friggin' neck, the double dealer! You just fix that ranger, if you're fucking up to it, Ettore. 'Cause if you aren't . . .'

Simone had let out a burp, and the line went dead.

He was nervous, Ettore realised.

Simone always burped when he was nervous.

As if he wasn't spouting enough hot air already.

Ettore stared at the phone for a moment, as though it might translate into clearer terms what he'd just heard from Simò, then he slipped the mobile in his pocket, crossed the street and walked into the Butterfly restaurant.

He didn't wait for a waitress to show him to a table, just sat down near the door.

Cangio recognised him the instant he walked in.

That tattoo on the side of his neck beneath his left ear.

Didn't he realise that Cangio was there?

That man had been driving the Mercedes with Antonio Marra riding in the back seat. He had probably murdered Maria Gatti. Maybe he'd blown Marzio's head off, too. An 'Ndrangheta hitman with a lizard tattoo exactly like that one had tried and failed to put a bullet through his brain the summer before last on Soverato beach.

Was it the same man, or another member of the same clan?

Did it make any difference?

He'd been planning to speak with Mister Butterfly, sleep in the airport lounge that night, catch the first flight back to Assisi the following morning, then report what he had learnt about Chinese truffles to Grossi and Esposito, and let them work it out for themselves.

Now, someone was blocking the way.

If Lizard Man had trailed him to London, planning to kill him, there could only be one end to the story. His corpse would be found before the night was out – headless, maybe – in some dark alley, with a bullet in the back, or a knife in the heart.

Think wolf, he told himself.

'Truffled Chicken,' Mister Butterfly announced proudly.

The waitress came, a skinny bitch, black shirt and pants with a yellow Butterfly badge on her left tit.

She mumbled something Ettore didn't understand, then handed him a menu. Maybe she was moaning about the fact he'd grabbed the empty table next to the door without waiting to be asked.

He pointed to a bottle of beer on the next table, and she turned away and left him in peace. He opened the menu, glanced at the indecipherable Chinese characters and meaningless English words, and hoped the ranger would decide to leave before he needed to order anything.

Cangio was sitting at a table on a dais, talking with a Chinese man.

What was that all about, Ettore wondered.

An old friend?

He wondered if the Chinese would be attending Cangio's funeral.

FORTY-ONE

The chicken stuck like a ball in Cangio's throat.

He tried to cough the lump into the palm of his hand, but it wouldn't come.

His heart was pumping in places where it shouldn't be pumping. It throbbed in his forehead, pounded in his ears, while his chest was a dead zone, lungs blocked, neither rising nor falling.

A fist hit him hard in the ribs – Mister Butterfly's cure for a blocked oesophagus – and he managed to swallow and clear his throat.

'The truffled chicken was a bit dry,' Cangio apologised, his eyes watering, his face bright red as his breathing came back. 'That was quite a punch.'

The little man grinned as a waiter came running with a carafe of water. Cangio gulped down air, then followed it with water. Imagine choking to death with your would-be assassin looking on as you did the job for him.

He was probably safe while he was in the restaurant . . .

He remembered Soverato beach.

He wasn't safe, at all. That day, the 'Ndrangheta killer had walked down a beach full of children and parents, stuck a pistol in the face of a man who was sleeping beneath a sunshade, and pulled the trigger five times in front of hundreds of witnesses.

While he'd been choking, a different scene had flashed before his eyes.

It happened to people who were about to die, they said, and now he knew that it was true. They saw the past like a slide show, all the memorable moments in their lives flashed before them in the blinking of an eye.

London, the year before.

He'd be in another restaurant, an Indian one.

There was a way to get out of there alive.

If he'd had his pistol, he wouldn't have thought twice.

Pistols make a lot of noise. They frighten people. No man in his right mind tries to stop a man with a gun. He could have walked up and stuck it in the ranger's face, and everyone would have jumped out of the way. Out in the street, he could lose himself in the crowd in no time. But his gun was in Umbria. He might have got it through the control gate in the tiny airport of Assisi, but there was no way of knowing what might happen in terrorist-struck London.

Still, lack of a gun wasn't going to save the ranger.

He had killed people in lots of ways.

He'd have to improvise, wouldn't he?

He was looking around for a decent weapon when the rumpus began.

Cangio turned the table over.

Plates, knives, forks and glasses went flying.

He opened his mouth and started to shout.

All eyes turned, everyone watching him.

Mister Butterfly's eyes almost popped with shocked incomprehension as the dinner plopped into his lap. Dark-eyed waiters, blue-eyed customers. Eyes of every colour from every country on the planet were on him.

'This food is shit!' Cangio yelled like a Friday-night drunk. 'And as for these truffles . . .'

A waiter, braver than most, came running around the table to restrain him and Cangio punched him square on the jaw.

Next thing, the place was jumping.

*　　*　　*

Ettore cursed.

What the fuck was the bastard doing?

In two seconds, he had turned the place into a mad circus.

Half a dozen waiters and waitresses closed in on Cangio's table.

He could see the ranger standing on the dais, a head taller than any of Mister Butterfly's employees, his fists raised, threatening to punch anyone who came near him. The old man was wiping off his shiny suit with a white table napkin, looking like he was heading for a major heart seizure.

The waitress dumped a bottle of beer on Ettore's table, then ran out into the street.

He leant across, grabbed a razor-sharp meat knife from a tray of cutlery on the table by the door, sat down again. If Cangio tried to break out through the door, he'd be walking straight on to the blade.

A hard jolt struck his shoulder, knocking Ettore aside.

Two British bobbies in helmets and riot vests came charging into the restaurant.

He was thrown for a moment. He'd missed his chance. He'd be crazy to try anything while the cops were there.

He watched as Cangio held up his hands in surrender. The coppers grabbed his wrists, then they walked him towards the door and the street. They were no more than three steps apart, when Ettore saw the ghost of a smile on the ranger's lips.

Ettore slipped the knife into his pocket and followed them outside.

'What's all this about then, chum?'

They were standing in the street outside the restaurant. The policeman who had spoken had a chubby face, red cheeks, dark freckles and piercing green eyes.

Cangio didn't say a word to explain himself.

He wanted to be arrested, wanted to be driven fast and safe out of Soho in the back of a Black Maria. He would have liked nothing better than to be locked up in a police cell for the night. To have the chance of speaking with a senior officer, explain what he was doing in London, asking him to phone Perugia and confirm what he had said with the RCS captains. It was a golden opportunity. Anything was better than dying.

The other bobby leant close, sniffed his breath. 'It's the drink.

You can smell it. He's been drinking something fancy, if you ask me.'

Cangio could have told them it was the stink of Chinese truffles, but he didn't.

'He doesn't look drunk to me,' the first one said. 'What's your name?'

Cangio pulled out his passport, showed it to the man.

'Italian, are you? On your own? There's worse trouble than him knocking around tonight,' the bobby said to his mate. He handed Cangio his passport back, watched him put it away in his jacket. 'I bet the grub was lousy, right? Go on, then, piss off, will you.'

The other man flared up. 'Are you letting him go?'

'He got his free meal, didn't he? Go on, fuck off!'

The policeman turned away, and his mate went after him.

Cangio found himself standing alone on the pavement.

Facing the man with the lizard tattoo.

Cangio turned and ran like hell.

The ranger darted through the crowd, head down, feinting left and right, nippy as a mountain goat, but keeping a straight line like a rugby player heading for the try line.

Ettore wasn't used to running, he could barely keep up. Physical exercise was something you did in jail. The crowd was getting thicker too, more people pouring into Chinatown all the time, heading for the restaurants.

Ettore thought he'd lost him, then he caught sight of the ranger.

There was heavy traffic on the main road.

Ettore saw him stop, look back, then dart across the road and down a staircase.

FORTY-TWO

I f wolves had been so dumb, they'd be extinct.

He was running down the wrong escalator staircase.

Instead of heading up to Angel via the Piccadilly line on a train full of people going to a place full of pubs, cinemas and restaurants, he was on the Bakerloo line heading south. Away from the city centre, far from the crowds, and into an area that was an abandoned no man's land by night once you left the roundabout and the buses behind.

Fear had forced him into making an error.

He heard sharp footsteps on the moving metal stairs above him, a train pulling in on the track below. He leapt the last few steps, then raced down the platform alongside the emptying carriages, only hopping on the Tube the instant the doors let out a hiss as they got ready to shut.

He caught his breath, then turned around.

Lizard Man was in the carriage behind him, staring at him through the plate glass of the dividing door, watching his every move, like a snake closing in on a cornered prey before it struck the fatal blow.

If he had come to London with murder in mind, he must be armed. With a gun, perhaps. He must have had friends at Assisi airport to smuggle a weapon on to an aeroplane. Did he have friends in London, too, who might be supplying backup?

And yet, the man seemed to be alone.

Then another thought flashed through his mind.

Did Lizard Man know London better than he did?

As the train picked up speed and rocked on the rails, he wondered why the 'Ndrangheta hadn't tried to kill him in Umbria. Had they been too busy taking care of Marzio, Maria Gatti and anyone else who had stood in the way of what they were doing?

And had his own turn now arrived?

As the train braked hard and rattled into Embankment, the Lizard Man stepped out quickly onto the platform, blocking his escape, one hand holding onto the open door while he waited for Cangio to make a move, jumping back on the train as the doors hissed and it prepared to depart.

If he had a gun, why didn't he use it?

The same thing happened at Waterloo, and again at Lambeth North, a sort of cat-and-mouse contest, Lizard Man taunting him, daring him to make a run for it, while he hung back, unwilling to take the risk.

Was the killer nervous about using a weapon on the

Underground, afraid of being caught on an empty platform, alone with a corpse and the smoking gun in his hand?

The tannoy sounded, and a tinny voice filled the near-empty carriage: *This train will terminate at Elephant & Castle.*

Was that the plan?

Get him to Elephant and Castle, then terminate *him*?

Three minutes later, the train pulled in at the end of the line. Lizard Man darted out onto the platform and took up his blocking position again, as if expecting the train to depart.

Hadn't he heard the announcement?

Or hadn't he understood it?

Cangio took his chance – he could only go left – and found himself running in the direction of the yellow *Way Out* sign.

Had Lizard Man been dreaming?

Or was he a stranger in London?

He was halfway up the escalator before he risked a look back.

The hunter was down at the bottom of the staircase. He had paused, looking around as if to find his bearings, then spotted him.

Cangio sprinted upwards, onwards, for the street.

Elephant and Castle.

Exits east, west and south.

He knew the area a bit, but not that well.

Which exit had he taken when he was working at Death Row?

That was what another Italian dishboy had called the greasy spoon where Cangio had survived for a couple of weeks after arriving in London the first time. He had spent his time washing dishes all day long in water that was never hot and rarely changed, wiping cups and plates with a dishcloth that stood up on its own without any help. The place might still exist, though by now it would be closed for the day.

South?

He heard footsteps closing in, and dashed in that direction, hoping to lose the Lizard Man in the maze of pedestrian tunnels.

If he could just manage to skip on a bus.

He'd sometimes taken the number twelve to the West End after work, though plenty of bus routes passed through Elephant and Castle. Any bus would do, a bus going anywhere, just so long as it carried him away and left Lizard Man behind without a ride.

Panic drove all memories out of his head.
He ran for his life.

He had to keep Cangio in sight.

He had no idea where they were.

The ranger had an advantage on him there. He'd lived in London.

Cangio pushed his ticket through the electronic barrier, kept on running.

Ettore vaulted the barrier, kept on chasing, despite the shout behind him, 'Oi, you! Where's your bloody ticket!'

Was that why Don Michele hadn't trusted him after the killing at Soverato beach? 'You'll get yourself in trouble,' the don had told him when he'd offered to follow the ranger to London and kill him there. 'Wait 'til he comes home, Ettò, they always do.'

Cangio went charging down a tunnel like a hare out of a trap, and Ettore went after him.

Did Cangio have friends in that part of town? Was that the plan? A place to disappear? If he lost the ranger now, he was in trouble, and he knew it. Don Michele would crush him like an insect. Lose the ranger, he wouldn't be going home.

He'd have no home to go to.

He had to get closer.

One jab with the knife he'd nicked from the Chinese restaurant, a sharp thrust into the small of his back, pushing up towards the ranger's lungs and heart, and that was that.

Desperation was driving him, he was gaining ground.

Use the knife, he told himself, there'd be nothing to be desperate about.

FORTY-THREE

Cangio broke into the fading daylight, streetlights fighting the gloom.

And there was Death Row – *Giovanni's Cafeteria*, the sign proudly proclaimed.

Merda!

He'd found the café, but the bus stop he wanted was on the far side of the roundabout.

There were buses pulling in, others pulling away, but he was on the wrong side of the busy junction. He'd been hoping to jump on a bus that would take him back towards Trafalgar Square and Chinatown, leaving Lizard Man in the lurch.

He hadn't finished talking with Mister Butterfly.

They still had more to tell each other . . .

The killer came bursting out of the pedestrian walkway.

Something glistened in his fist as the metal caught the light. There was no escape.

Except . . .

Instinct kicked in.

A number twelve was approaching the bus stop.

A tried and trusted friend. When he finished work at Death Row, he would climb aboard, say good evening to the driver, show his ticket, then add, 'Take me home, Battista,' as if the bus were a limousine, and the driver was his personal chauffeur.

'Save my skin, Battista!' he breathed quietly.

There was a way. He'd done it before, vaulted the metal safety barrier and sprinted across the wide road, ignoring the traffic. Once he'd been hit by a man on a bicycle. 'That'll teach you!' the cyclist had shouted. 'Fucking pedestrians, you don't know your arse from your tits!'

Cangio didn't hesitate.

Think wolf!

He followed his instincts.

He was three metres short when the ranger jumped.

Three metres short of ramming the knife into the ranger's kidneys, and ending the farce. Once the blade sank home, it was a question of ripping with all your might, severing anything that got in the way until you hit something vital. The shock was always fatal. Then all he'd have to do was drop the knife, walk away and jump on the first bus that came along. Then take a taxi to the airport, and he'd be eating breakfast in Italy.

But the ranger was gone.

Ettore vaulted the guardrail in pursuit, glancing left, and then it hit him.

In both senses.

Fuck me, he thought in a moment of blind panic, that bus is going the wrong way.

As the N133 came roaring round the corner on its way to Brixton, 'Battista' didn't have time to hit the brakes.

The noise was terrific.

A loud thump, a clang of metal, the popping squelch of something bursting open.

Brakes screeched and car horns blared as Cangio stopped and turned to see what had happened.

There were people standing in front of the bus, fists to mouths, the driver covering his face with his hands.

Cangio took a deep breath as he ran back across the road and stared down at the man who had been trying to kill him.

Lizard Man lay twisted in the gutter, his body crushed beneath the nearside wheel, his neck now bent and broken, blood seeping from his nose and his ears, the blue tattoo replaced by a raw red gash.

Then a mobile phone trilled in the dead man's jacket.

Cangio dropped down on one knee, pushed his hand into the Lizard Man's pocket.

'Hey!' someone objected.

'He's Italian,' Cangio said. 'I speak Italian.'

He checked the name on the display – *Simone Candelora* – and pressed the answer button.

'What the fuck are you playing at?'

It had taken Ettore ages to answer the phone.

'Is your battery flat, or something?' Candelora shouted, his voice louder than usual, England being so far away.

The *sì* that came back was barely audible.

He wondered whether Ettore had been drinking.

'I can't find fucking Marra,' Candelora growled, 'but when I do, he'll wish he'd never been born. I've looked all over for him. If he's on the run, let's hope he doesn't find his way to the fucking *carabinieri* . . . Ettore, are you listening to me?'

The silence lengthened.

Ettore might be busy, hunting down the ranger.

'Did you waste him in the restaurant, then?'

'*Sì.*'

'OK, then. Text me when you get to the airport.'

Candelora ended the call and cursed. That twit was close to getting things dusted in London, a place he didn't know, while he was stuck in the backwoods of fucking Umbria to no good purpose.

If Marra talked, the entire operation was blown.

He didn't want to think about it.

He had to find Marra.

Fast.

Cangio slipped the Lizard Man's phone in his pocket.

He put his hand on the shoulder of the bus driver. 'It wasn't your fault,' he said. 'We all saw what happened. This man was Italian, a tourist. It was his first time in England, apparently; he didn't know which way the traffic flows. An unlucky accident.'

'Thanks,' the driver murmured. 'I've called the police. There were plenty of witnesses. I hope you'll tell them what you saw?'

'Of course,' Cangio said, drawing back into the crowd.

He waited a minute, then vaulted the metal barrier again, and took the tunnel heading for the Tube station and the taxi rank.

There was no one else waiting.

'The Butterfly restaurant, Gerrard Street,' he said as he boarded a cab.

If his luck held, he wouldn't need to spend much time with Mister Butterfly. Just a quick apology and a brief conversation, that's *if* his luck held out. With a bit more luck, he might even catch the evening flight back to Italy.

So far, he had been very, very lucky.

FORTY-FOUR

C andelora closed the garage door, then switched on the light.

The loading bay was empty; there was no sign of the Porsche 911. Not that he had been expecting to find it parked there anyway. If Marra was trying to avoid him, he would have left the car out in the woods, on the truffle reserve most likely, then made his way to the factory on foot.

If that was where he was hiding.

Had Rosanna been telling the truth over the phone when she said that Marra had gone home, or had the secretary been covering for him? Marra's house had been empty, that was for sure. The imbecile might be anywhere by now. In Perugia, even, talking to the *carabinieri*.

Unless he'd decided to grab the cash and make a run for it.

Talk about a fly gumming up the works.

Thank God he'd blocked the evening's delivery. He had made a phone call, told the lads who were driving the vans to sleep over in the motel outside Frosinone, south of Rome. 'There are too many bluebottles on the road up here tonight. Same time, same place tomorrow, OK?'

By tomorrow, he hoped to have things straightened out.

Three minutes later, Don Michele had called, which came as no surprise.

Simone had known that one of the drivers would pass it on.

'What's going on, Simò?'

No preliminaries – 'how are things', 'how's life', 'everything all right, Simò?' – straight to the point.

He knew he'd have to play this right, make sure the don didn't call up Ettore to double-check. If Dick Brain didn't tell him straight away, he'd have let it slip out sooner or later that he was in London.

'Nothing much, Don Michè. Just being cautious.'

'Don't play the saint with me, Simò. The vans, the loads. You've got them stopped off south of Rome. Why's that?'

'I told the drivers, didn't I? Too much action in the area, flashing blue lights, know what I mean? What difference does a day make? Tomorrow it will have all blown over.'

There had been silence at the other end of the line.

The boss hadn't fallen for it.

'They're still pretty busy, tidying up loose ends, Don Michè.'

'Over that fucking witch? Still hanging onto the Devil's tail, are they?'

Simone had laughed, letting the don know he'd hit the bull's eye.

'The Prince of Darkness is still number one on the wanted list,' Simone had reassured him, 'though there's been a bit of fuss over some bones a farmer found when a pack of wolves had a go at his sheep. Turns out they're human. The bones, mind, not the sheep.'

It was always best to throw in a healthy dollop of truth when talking with Don Michele. He'd be sitting at his desk down in Calabria with copies of the Umbrian newspapers spread out in front of him.

'They're from years back, probably Asian,' Simone had added. 'That's what the cops are saying. Didn't you spot it in the papers, Don Michè?'

He must have read about it, because he didn't say a word.

'Are things going to the dogs up there, Simò?' Don Michele had said at last.

It had taken Simone a bit to sort his voice out, find the right bounce, the right tone. 'It's full steam ahead in Umbria, Don Michè. Nothing here to worry about. One night won't change a thing, will it?'

'Make sure it doesn't.'

As the phone went dead, Simone Candelora had reached for the plastic bottle of water on the bedside table. He'd emptied it in three or four gulps, his throat as scorched as a baker's oven. It was never easy talking to Don Michele. And when he had to lie to him, it brought on an acid heartburn that ravaged his guts. There was only one way to cure it.

He had to find Marra.

Marra hadn't learnt from the bungee jump. He hadn't learnt from the death of the witch. Even Ettore kicking the shit out of him had done no good. It was time to get serious. Antonio Marra was going to scream tonight until his voice ran out.

Punishment wasn't the word for what he was going to get, the trouble he was causing.

Simone climbed the stairs from the underground garage to the ground floor, fingering his keys in the dark to find the one that opened the reinforced door. He'd taken the decision to change the locks when Marra started harping on about wanting to drop out of the business. If the bastard ever did decide to run with a bit of dodgy paperwork in his briefcase, he'd have to break into his own factory and crack his own safe first.

Marra knew what they were doing, but he wouldn't be able to prove a thing without evidence. He'd have made a piss poor eyewitness in any case, hiding away in his office whenever a consignment turned up, just signing his name on the dotted line, then charging off home.

What was that big bird called, the one that buried its head in the sand?

Marra's head was in so deep, all you could see was his arse.

He felt his anger building as he crossed the hall, the night-lights dim and gloomy.

It was clear now, wasn't it? Marra had *known* what was going on when those bones had been dug up. That was the day he'd turned up at the bungee jumping park in Ferentillo, telling them he wanted to pull out of the partnership.

Merda!

He blamed himself. He should have realised there was some-thing behind it. Instead of shaking the truth out of him there and then, he'd played with him. He'd put Marra's fright down to the fact that he was new to the game, worried about the heavy police presence in the area, the idea that one of their vans might get stopped.

Marra had made a fool of *him*. And he *still* didn't know what secret the joker was hiding.

That truly put the wind up him.

Had he made an error choosing Marra Truffles for the drug-refining operation in Umbria?

A *fatal* error?

Tonight he was going to find out, then fix it.

Don Michele would never need to know.

First, he had a look in Marra's office.

The door was locked, but that was no problem for a man with all the keys.

He switched the light on, checked the safe: the stacks of cash and company papers were still intact. Marra hadn't managed to open it, even if he had tried. Next, the en suite toilet. He wasn't hiding there, and the window was locked from the inside. He checked the desk in case Marra had left some clue to where he might be going, what he was up to.

Nothing.

The big padded chair was pushed back from the desk, as if someone had been sitting there, but it could have been like that since the day before. The pens and papers on the desk were all in order. Rosanna's doing, no doubt. There were a couple of bills, some receipts, a statement from the local bank showing a nice healthy surplus, a hefty deposit to a bank down in Catanzaro that Don Michele often used.

Payment for a consignment of truffles.

He almost laughed out loud as he read it.

They'd really set this little fucker back in saddle. Just look at the cheques Don Michele's frontmen had sent him. When had Antonio Marra ever been so rich? Marra had known from the start that they were into more than fucking truffles. Who did he think he was working with, the holy nuns? Driven by greed and ambition, Marra had always wanted to be bigger than Luxuria Truffles, the major player in Valnerina. Instead, the loser had been dogged by bad luck and incapacity for years. Until Simone and the don had come along, Antonio Marra had never sold a truffle outside Italy.

Now, it was time for Marra to clear up all the mystery, and bow out of the business for good.

Candelora stopped his searching and listened.

He'd heard the muffled rasp of metal on concrete, something being dragged. If it wasn't in the loading bay, it could only be coming from the production department down in the basement where the truffles were cleaned and dried by day, and where the coke and truffle sauce was fed into the empty glass jars once the workers had gone home.

He switched off the office lights, went out into the hall.

He stood in the gloom for a moment, waiting to hear the noise again.

Instead, he heard a different sound, like a groan or a stifled cough.

The *carabinieri*?

His blood ran cold at the idea.

Then he thought of Maria Gatti.

She'd called up the spirits of the dead, Marra had told him. He'd sworn that he had heard them himself, even after Maria had gone home and left him on his own in the factory.

Simone forced himself to think of Don Michele.

The don would turn *him* into a fucking spirit if he didn't get things sorted fast.

He went charging downstairs, making no effort to be silent. *Carabinieri*, ghosts, or Antonio Marra, he would deal with each one as the opportunity presented itself.

He pushed the sliding doors aside, stepped into the room, and his heart stopped.

The figure silhouetted against the window had very little that was human about it. A vast body, a tiny head, one arm reaching up towards the latch, like some sort of movie alien, a thin desperate hiss of a voice.

'Fucking hell, fucking hell, open, for the love of Christ!'

He flicked the light switch and the neon came to life in a blinding flash.

Antonio Marra was crouching on the conveyor belt, half hidden by the truffle feeder, trying desperately to open the window and make his escape.

'What's the rush, Antò? All you had to do was use the door.'

Marra turned and looked at him, eyes wild and startled, then he turned back to the window, rattling the latch again, beating his fist against the glass, getting nowhere. There was a stink of truffles in the place, and something else, too, as if he'd done it in his pants.

'I'm off, Simone. You gotta let me go. I'm getting out. It's yours, all yours.'

Then he was back at the window, hammering on the glass as if some friendly soul on the other side might open it for him.

'You've got some explaining to do, you prick! What's all this about sheep and bones?'

Marra didn't answer the question.

'I'm away, Simò. Just let me go. You'll never hear of me again. I tried to tell you, but you wouldn't listen. That day in Ferentillo, the bungee jumping—'

'What the fuck have you done?'

Simone moved in on him. Marra raised his hands to protect

his face, then he tripped and fell off the conveyor belt. He didn't make a sound as he hit his shoulder with a crunch on the concrete floor. 'You don't want to know,' he said. 'It's better for you. You can't tell the coppers what you don't know—'

'*What* don't I know?'

Marra's voice was a whining sing-song. When he wasn't speaking, he was mumbling, saying the same things over and over. He had to go. It was better for them. He was really sorry. He had to go.

'Sorry for *what*?' Simone shouted, standing over him, towering above him.

'They won't come looking for you or Ettore. It's me they're after. Me.'

Simone's foot shot out and caught the side of Marra's face.

Marra moaned and spat out blood, but he wouldn't shut up. 'I gotta run, Simò. I'm telling you. I'm just a dead weight.'

'Let me decide. Maybe I can help you. What's it all about?'

Marra's shoulders were jiving, jerking up and down, as if he was crying, as if he couldn't breathe, though it didn't stop him yapping on. 'Let me out, Simò, I gotta run.'

Simone grabbed his hair and heaved him to his feet. There was blood on his face, one eye leaking, and something white that might have been a bit of tooth sticking out of his bottom lip.

'You can keep the lot,' Marra wailed. 'I haven't taken anything. Papers, money, nothing. I swear to you. I'm begging you, Simò, just let me go . . .'

Like a broken record, over and over.

Simone almost admired his nerve, the stubborn way he stuck to his guns.

Who would have thought the worm had it in him? Whatever he might have done, he'd kept quiet about it. He'd never let on, or given a hint that anything was wrong.

'Stop fucking whining! I want answers.'

Wanted them? *Needed* them, that was the truth.

If the cops caught Marra, and he started this routine, they'd stick him in a cell and grill him for as long as it took. He'd tell them the lot. The bones, the sheep, Marra Truffles, his new partners from Calabria, his recent developments in the international truffle trade.

Don Michele would not be pleased.

He would not be pleased at all.

FORTY-FIVE

H e made it by a whisker.

Seb Cangio was the last passenger to board the 20.20 flight to Perugia.

As the plane lifted off, tilting upwards into the sky, he relaxed for the first time since leaving London. He was going home sooner than planned, but now he had the answer he'd been looking for.

The Lizard Man's mobile phone had been a goldmine of information, and he had made good use of it on the train to Stansted airport. The dead man's name was Ettore Pallucchi. He was from Pentone, a small town in Calabria that Cangio remembered from his student days. He had sometimes stopped there for coffee and a sandwich while monitoring the wolf population in the nearby Sila mountains. There were more 'Ndrangheta clans in the Sila foothills, they said, than midges in a stagnant summer pond.

Ettore talked on a daily basis with Simone Candelora, the man who had phoned while he had been kneeling beside Ettore's lifeless body after the accident at the Elephant and Castle. The two men spoke to each other a dozen times a day, and they often swapped phone messages, most of them concerning Marra Truffles. The truffle processing plant played a major part in what they were doing, and they often arranged to meet there. The odd thing about these meetings was that they usually took place when the factory was closed.

What the hell did they do there at three o'clock in the morning?

He had himself seen lorries driving into the plant at night. Marra Truffles was expanding, people said.

Well, now he could guess what Marra had been expanding into.

As he shuffled forward at the boarding gate, he'd sent a message from Ettore's phone to Simone Candelora, using a phrase he had poached from a gangster film: *The ranger's sleeping with the fishes. See you at MT after midnight.*

At that point, he had switched off Ettore's phone.

Then he had sent a similar message to another recipient from his own mobile: *Be at Marra Truffles at midnight tonight. I'll be waiting there.* He signed it *Cangio* before he pressed the send button. As he presented his ticket and prepared to board the plane, he had disconnected his own phone, too, as flight regulations requested.

He closed his eyes, settled back against the head-rest.

Mister Butterfly had been surprised to see him.

'I'll call the police again,' he had said.

'I'm not drunk,' Cangio had reassured him. 'I wasn't drunk before.'

He'd apologised and told Li Liü Gong that a man had been trying to kill him.

'I'm not surprised,' the Chinese man had said.

Then Li Liü Gong had told him what he had meant earlier that evening, when he had spoken of 'an experience' he wouldn't wish to repeat with a customer from Umbria.

'I have no proof,' Li Liü Gong said, 'but I have no doubt of it.'

Cangio had no doubt of it either, and now he had the proof in his pocket.

He opened his eyes as the hostess passed along the aisle with a trolley selling refreshments. He bought a beer and a ham sandwich.

His thoughts turned to Sibillines National Park where he worked. The landscape was breathtaking. The medieval towns and villages enshrined a way of life that had changed very little through the centuries. People raised sheep, planted orchards, searched the woods for truffles and mushrooms. The forests and mountains provided refuge for an incredible range of animals, birds and plants.

It was no exaggeration to call it paradise, though a dark pall of fear and death had been cast over everything. And it had all started with Marzio's 'strange sightings' in the forest near Vallo di Nera two years before.

He swallowed the remains of his sandwich and washed it down with beer.

The plane would be landing within an hour.

The hunt for the truth wasn't over.

Not yet.

FORTY-SIX

H e couldn't move.

His hands were free, but his wrists and ankles were tied fast.

He could shift his eyes, but he couldn't move his head. A rubber strap was crushing down against his forehead, holding him fixed and immobile, stretched out on his back.

He had had a cancer scare a couple of years back, the full works, CAT scans, biopsies. He was reminded of that experience, getting ready to go into the scanning machine like a man laid out on a rack before the torture started. He mustn't move a fraction, they had told him before the scanner started making grinding noises, or they'd need to do it all again.

The only difference was the dangling rubber tube in his mouth.

The tube didn't hurt, but he couldn't get rid of it, couldn't spit it out.

He felt the urge to gag, sure he was going to choke on it, as the panic built up in blinding waves.

'Comfortable?' a voice said, and a head moved into focus.

Simone Candelora. It all came back.

Simone had found him hiding in the processing room. Simone was out of his mind with anger, asking questions, punching him when he didn't answer. He must have blacked out, and Candelora had bound him to the conveyor belt with packing tape while he was unconscious.

'Let's start again, shall we?'

Start again? He couldn't say a word with the tube in his mouth. Then he heard a click – the feeder button – and saw the black paste snaking down the transparent plastic tube. The air pushed back into his throat and lungs, the pressure building up as the oily truffle paste came spurting out of the tube.

'Tasty, eh?' Candelora said.

Marra struggled to breathe, his nose and mouth filling up with truffle sauce, choking on the stuff, trying to cough it out, then having to swallow, and swallow, and swallow again. It was that, or nothing. Swallow or die.

Candelora pushed the button and ripped the plastic tube from his mouth.

He leant close, his eyes like burning coals. 'Unless you tell me what I want to know, Antò, you won't be here to talk tomorrow. I've got everything I need in this fucking room. I've got cutters, grinders, mixers, bottles, packing machines. I can send you out of here in a cardboard carton in forty glass jars marked *Marra* fucking *Truffles*.'

Cangio was on the hillside, staring through his night vision glasses.

He wasn't watching the wolves tonight, though. It had taken just half an hour to drive there from the airport. The factory car park was empty, which was no surprise. He had told them to be there at midnight, but who was ever on time in Italy? The truffle processing plant was dark, apparently empty, with dimmed night-lights here and there, and a couple of bright red dots that might have been fire or burglar alarm systems.

The place looked deserted, no sign of a watchman or a security guard.

And then he heard a noise.

The night was full of noises, hooting owls, whistling bats, unexpected rustles in the undergrowth, but this was something grinding and mechanical, a machine of some sort.

It went on for a minute or so, a distant humming, coming from Marra Truffles.

Was something programmed to switch itself on and off at certain hours of the night? A fridge or a boiler, maybe.

He started running across the hillside, the stubble shimmering in the moonlight like a million tiny metal blades where the grass had been cropped short by grazing sheep. He wanted to check the rear of the factory before he moved any closer.

*   *   *

'What's all this about Chinamen, Antò?'

Antonio Marra puked up some more truffle paste. He looked a right fucking mess, as if he'd grown an oily black beard. He stank of garlic and truffles.

Marra stared up at him. 'Chinamen?' he managed to say, still playing for time, still thinking he could pull the wool over the sheep's eyes.

'You heard me! What's the story?'

He held the feeder tube in front of Marra's face and saw his eyes light up with terror. 'And just remember this, Antò. I want the truth.'

'I don't know what you mean.'

He pushed the plastic tube into the silly fucker's mouth and pressed the red feeder button again.

Cangio ran for a hundred metres.

He dropped down on one knee, aimed his binoculars on the back of the factory.

The same red dots of light were visible on the first floor, but to the right on the lower floor, he saw a narrow strip of light where a blind had been left open. All the other blinds were closed, the windows dark. Had someone gone home, forgetting to switch off the lights and pull down the shades?

He swept the building from one end to the other through the night-glasses, the contrast ranging from sparkling pinpoints of lime to murky bars of near-black where the limited infra-red spectrum failed. There was a door at one end of the building. Taller and wider than a normal door, it looked like a service entrance with a smooth metal shutter which rolled up and down, probably propelled by an electric motor. The door wasn't shut. Not quite.

There was a strip of impenetrable darkness at the bottom.

Someone was inside the factory.

'Let me go, Simò. I need to puke . . . ukh!'

'This Chinaman was working for you. OK, and so?'

'An accident. That's what happened. He had an accident.'

'And you got rid of him?'

'Let me up, Simò, for Chrissakes! It was me—'

'You buried him in the woods.'

There was no way out of it. Lies, and more lies, otherwise the bastard would kill him.

'Yeah, yeah.'

'I didn't think you had it in you, Antò. Hang on a bit, though. How did you do it? That's what I can't figure. I mean to say, did you bring him here to do the cutting and snipping, or did you do it out in the woods with an axe or something?'

That stumped him. 'I . . . I . . .' he murmured. 'I couldn't bring him here, Simò.'

Candelora reached for the plastic tube, held it up in front of his eyes.

'Tell me how you did it. Exactly how. The details, everything.'

Holy Christ, he thought, if the *carabinieri* ever get a hold of this . . .

Cangio crawled beneath the open door, pulled himself to his feet.

He was in an ample loading bay that doubled as a garage.

There was a black Mercedes parked inside, no sign of Marra's Porsche. That Mercedes . . . He'd seen it coming down from Cerreto the day Maria Gatti was found. He had nearly crashed into it. The Mercedes driven by Ettore Pallucchi, the *'Ndranghetista*, who was dead in London.

The other man must be in the factory . . .

The one who'd been in the car with Ettore Pallucchi and Marra.

Were they getting ready to celebrate with Ettore?

That's who they were expecting. After the message he'd sent from Ettore's mobile phone – *See you at MT after midnight* – they'd be waiting for Ettore to come back and tell them how he had murdered the park ranger in London, celebrating over a bottle of champagne, or something.

As he opened the inner door on the far side of the garage and stepped into the corridor, someone screamed.

'What the hell do you think he's up to?'

'We'll find out when we get there,' Lucia Grossi said. 'How much longer?'

'I don't know precisely. Five, ten minutes?'

They raced through Sellano on the twisty old SP459 from Foligno. A shortcut to Valnerina, Jerry Esposito had said, but the narrow road kept winding back on itself.

'We should have brought the riot mob,' Esposito said. 'Just the two of us? He could be armed.'

'If you ask me, he wants to surrender, hand himself in. He's already looking at life – two murders, Diamante and Gatti – plus those unexplained bones. He'd be mad to try and shoot his way out.'

'If he thinks surrendering will earn him remission, he's got another think coming.'

'Step on it,' Lucia Grossi urged him. 'And mind you don't kill anything.'

There were metal signs at hundred-metre intervals showing leaping deer.

At last they had entered the area of the national park.

Cangio moved along the corridor in the gloom.

The burglar alarms were false.

At least they didn't go off.

He stopped and listened at every door.

Nothing, nothing, nothing.

He reached the last door, put his ear to the wood and heard a voice, and another noise of some sort. That grinding sound again. Then a cry of protest.

There were at least two people in the factory, and one of them didn't sound happy.

He glanced at his watch. Two minutes to midnight. He should have waited in the car park for the RCS, but you couldn't ignore those screams. If he could just create a bit of confusion, the Twelfth Cavalry were bound to arrive. Sooner rather than later, he hoped, as he turned the handle, pushed the door and stepped silently into the processing room.

A tall man was standing over Antonio Marra.

Marra was stretched out on a conveyor belt, strapped to it with silver ducting tape, a long plastic tube sticking into his mouth.

Marra's eyes goggled at the sight of possible rescue. The man turned round, stared at him for an instant, then pulled a pistol

from the waistband of his trousers. He stretched out his right
arm, pointing the gun.

'Fuck me!' he said. 'Are you a ghost, or what?'

Cangio dived behind a work bench and a shot rang out.

'What happened to Ettore?' the man called out.

'Ettore sends his apologies,' Cangio shouted back.
'Unfortunately, he couldn't come tonight. He fell in love with
London. He's staying in a nice hotel. They call it The Mortuary.'

He heard the sound of footsteps, but he wasn't sure where
they were coming from.

Had his luck exhausted itself in London?

He had parked his van outside Marra Truffles.

It was 00.02 as he approached the building. It shouldn't be more
than a three-minute stop, just to check the main door and the
delivery door at the back. The front door was locked, as a solid
rattle of the handle confirmed. He peered through the glass and
looked down the long dimly lit corridor. All was as quiet as usual.

At the back of the building he got a bit of a surprise.

The loading door hadn't been properly closed.

Or had it been forced open?

He crawled under the door, and saw the Mercedes parked
inside. One of the owners, he imagined. He could hear voices
coming from the production department. A big order, maybe they
were working late.

Should he leave them to it?

He shook his head, smiled to himself. OK, being a night-
watchman wasn't a well-paid or glamorous job, but it was a job,
and you did what you had to do. He couldn't just pretend that
he hadn't heard the voices, he had to go through and check.

He knocked on the connecting door, pushed it open, and a
man pointed a gun at him.

It had never happened to him before. Eleven years as a
watchman checking shops, banks and other business premises at
night, making sure the doors were locked, slipping a receipt ticket
under the door, then moving on to the next one.

He had a registered Colt revolver in his holster, but he had
never fired it, except on the shooting range. Maybe it was the
fact that someone was pointing a gun at him.

His hand went to unclip the button on his holster when the other man fired.

He used what cover he could and began to move.

He crept towards the door the dead man had come through.

It must lead straight to the garage. The security guard was sprawled on the floor, flat on his back, a pool of blood spreading out around his head, the shiny black butt of a pistol lolling half out of the holster on his Sam Browne belt.

He made a feint towards the gun.

Candelora fired. The bullet pinged off metal, went zinging around the room, dinging off something else, then shattered through glass.

Cangio ignored the gun, skipped over the body and bolted for the door that led to the corridor. He turned left, running for the main entrance, heard the gunman close behind him, heard another sharp crack, another miss, the bullet ricocheting off the walls around his ears.

He reached the door, saw figures out in the car park, moving fast towards the door.

Candelora fired again, and the plate glass door collapsed in a shower of fragments.

Think wolf, he told himself, holding up his hands, turning around.

'Don't shoot,' he shouted.

Jerry Esposito came flying in through the broken door, pistol in hand.

Both guns exploded in the corridor. Esposito groaned and fell to the floor.

Cangio tried not to think of the *carabiniere*.

He blocked Esposito out of his mind.

Think wolf! he told himself. *Survive!*

He had to close the distance, then attack at the first opportunity.

Candelora moved towards him, levelling the gun, holding it two-handed, sideways, the way they did in recent movies when mobsters were executing mobsters.

'Drop that pistol!' a voice shouted, as a figure burst in through the door that led to the garage.

The voice was firm and strong.

A female voice.

Candelora fired again.

Lucia Grossi went down with a shriek, and he turned on Cangio.

'You bastard!' Candelora swore, baring his teeth.

The words were still ringing in the hallway as Esposito turned on his side, levelled his pistol and fired off a shot. Candelora collapsed against the wall, one side of his face blown off. His body slipped, then fell, his head bouncing on the rubberized tiling.

Lucia Grossi was back on her feet, moving in, covering the corpse, her gun in one hand, her phone in the other, blood pouring from the left shoulder of her uniform jacket.

'Agents down and wounded!' she shouted, and gave the coordinates of Marra Truffles. 'Multiple shooting. One dead, maybe more. We need a doctor, ambulances.'

Esposito had been shot in the hip. He was in pain, but he would live.

Candelora was beyond help, and no one was weeping.

'What about you?' she said, moving close to Cangio, her gun still pointing at the dead man on the floor.

'Are you always late?' he asked her. 'Another ten seconds, and he'd have killed me.'

Lucia Grossi looked down at him. Her lips stretched into a grin.

'We'll try to be later next time,' she said.

Then Cangio remembered the two men in the processing room.

FORTY-SEVEN

'I want you to start the ball rolling.'

Lucia Grossi had phoned him at seven thirty. The press conference was to be held that morning at *Carabinieri* Central Command in Perugia.

'I'll introduce you, then you kick in with the elves and the goblins,' she said. 'That'll grab their attention. All the rest follows on from there.'

'If you want fairy tales,' he said, 'I'll sit in the audience.'

'I want you on that stage,' she said. 'You've been in on this investigation from the start, and might have ended up on the pathologist's slab! They'll want to hear your account.'

'You were ready to arrest me yesterday,' he said.

That made her laugh. 'You did run off to London, remember?'

Cangio swallowed the words on his lips. *And wasn't it lucky for you that I did?*

He didn't want to argue with the woman. She had saved his life and risked her own in the process. Talking with her was like sniffing bleach, that was the problem. You knew you were going to end up getting burnt, feeling ill, or both.

'How's your arm?' he asked.

She ignored the question. 'Your face will be on all the front pages,' she said brightly. 'The ranger who saved the Umbrian truffle industry. Don't forget, Cangio, full uniform, please. You'll cut quite a figure.'

At 10.43 that morning, Cangio stood up as Lucia Grossi sat down.

He looked out over the auditorium as the TV camera lights came on, and microphones and iPads turned in his direction. Somewhere in the thick of the crowd a voice said clearly, 'Didn't they shoot him this time?'

Apart from the press, the room was packed with local politicians, high-ranking *carabinieri* officers with lots of gold braid and medals, the park director and the executive ranger. He had just spotted the pathologist Cristina di Marco, when he noticed Lori sitting quietly at the back of the room.

What was she doing there, he asked himself. Had she taken the day off work?

Lucia Grossi raised her finger at him, like a conductor to the first violin.

He gathered his notes together, then put them down again, feeling nervous, playing for time. Where should he begin? He still hadn't decided. Should he start with Antonio Marra, London, the 'Ndrangheta, the number of deaths involved?

Suddenly, he realised that Lucia Grossi was right.

Elves and goblins.

The journalists in the conference room wanted a story packed with mystery and blood. And if the 'Ndrangheta were thrown in for good measure, so much the better.

He took a deep breath.

'Strange sightings in the woods at dead of night,' he said. 'This case begins with the murder of a forest ranger who was investigating reports of ghostly apparitions. Marzio Diamante interviewed a number of witnesses who claimed to have seen such things two years before anyone else began to guess that something wasn't right in Umbria. Marzio paid for that knowledge with his life.'

He held up the papers in his hand as if they were Marzio's file.

'Strange creatures making unintelligible noises.'

He heard murmurs, one or two titters, but still the cameras flashed.

'Elves? Goblins? Legends? Folklore? No one took those stories seriously, except for Marzio Diamante.'

Let Marzio have his due, he thought. Let the 'Ndrangheta play second fiddle for the moment.

'Then one of the witnesses reported hearing a scream. And suddenly, the sightings ceased. Everything stopped two years ago . . .'

Cangio held the silence for several seconds. The audience shifted, as if they, too, felt safer in the knowledge that whatever had started was over and finished.

'The year before that, Marra Truffles had run into financial difficulties. The owner, Antonio Marra, was making efforts to salvage the company. And not merely salvage it. He wanted to turn it around. He hoped to move into the big time, and he thought he'd found a foolproof way of doing it.'

One of the journalists raised his hand.

As soon as he asked his question, Cangio knew he was a local man.

'Marra Truffles has never been big. Marra's reserves are relatively small. You can't just make truffles grow. Are you saying he'd found a Viagra pill for truffles?'

That caused quite a laugh.

Cangio raised a paper bag from the table. He held it up and the cameras flashed. They flashed again when he put his hand into the bag, and produced a small glass jar, which he held up to the assembly.

'This jar contains four truffles. Their scientific name is *Tuber himalayensis*. They look exactly like Umbrian truffles, the *Tuber melanosporum*, but they come from the province of Szechuan in China. The Chinese variety grows in remarkable quantities, and examples are sometimes unusually large. Viagra was mentioned a few moments ago . . .'

That raised another titter.

Cangio pointed to the front row. 'We are privileged to have two of the most experienced Umbrian truffle hunters here with us today, the Pastore brothers, Manlio and Teo, from Valnerina.'

The two men tried to sink red-faced into their seats, as Cangio went on, 'In their opinion, the Chinese truffle is a lethal danger to the prized and precious Umbrian truffle. These things,' he said, twirling the jar for the audience, 'are tasteless and have no aroma. In a word, they are of no commercial value. They are used to feed the pigs in China, though some are also used in local food preparation. Manlio Pastore calls them "poisonous spiders" and "aliens" that would wipe out our own autochthonous truffle species in next to no time.'

'That's why it's against the law to grow them,' Manlio Pastore growled.

'But if a man without scruples, and in financial difficulty, wanted to increase his own meagre production of truffles, the *Tuber himalayensis* is the answer to all his problems. All he has to do is pass them off as genuine Umbrian truffles. It's easily done, apparently, especially if the truffles are ground into a paste with anchovies and goat's milk—'

'Is that what Marra was doing?' Manlio asked in an angry voice.

'It's what he *would* have done, except for that scream in the night. Two years ago, Antonio Marra had come up with the scam, but he abandoned it almost immediately when something went wrong one night in the woods near his truffle reserve.'

'Screams in the night?' a journalist grumbled. Cangio remembered the same man creeping into his room in the hospital in

Spoleto six months earlier, and removing his oxygen mask so that he could talk about the 'Ndrangheta and the *carabiniere* general who had wanted him dead. 'I thought we were here to talk about organised crime?'

Cangio ignored him. 'That scream was made by a Chinese farmer who'd been planting truffles in the Marra truffle reserve. Marra had made contact with a Chinese businessman in London, and this go-between had found three expert truffle planters from Szechuan to work for Marra in secret. The Chinese spoke no Italian, and they worked only at night, but they didn't go unnoticed. Hunters and poachers saw them or heard them. They were small, agile, seen one instant, gone the next, disappearing into the woods. And so the legends of the elves and the gnomes began to spread.'

Cangio held up the jar of truffles again.

'This is the first crime of which Antonio Marra is accused: planting illegal tubers.'

'What about the scream?'

The query didn't come from the journalists, but from Cristina di Marco the pathologist, who was sitting in the front row.

Cangio stifled a smile. He knew what she was after. She wanted confirmation of the theory she had found on the Internet which said that Chinese jaws didn't 'rock'.

OK, Cristina di Marco would have her moment of triumph, too.

'The other week a human jawbone was found among the remains of a flock of sheep which had been massacred by wolves. Thanks to Dottoressa Cristina di Marco we now know that the jawbone, and a number of other bone fragments, belonged to one of the Chinese farm labourers who had been working for Antonio Marra.'

The pathologist sat back in her seat and let out a little whoop of triumph.

'*Dottoressa* di Marco,' Cangio said, directing his attention at her, 'your analysis of those bones revealed not only that they had been chopped into segments but also that there was a deep indentation in a fragment of thigh bone. I thought the indentations had been caused by wolves, while you held that the wolves had plenty of fresh meat to keep them busy.' He smiled, and bowed his head. 'You were correct. The Chinese worker had not been attacked by wolves. He had been attacked by a boar, whose tusks had left those marks in the thigh bone as they ripped through his femoral artery. The night the scream was heard, the three Chinese truffle planters had been charged by a herd of wild boar.'

'You mentioned chopping cuts,' the pathologist observed. 'They were not the work of a wild boar.'

'Certainly,' Cangio said, picking up the story again. 'There is no direct testimony of what happened that night, though it must have been a nightmarish scene. The three Chinese labourers had come to Italy with precise instructions. They'd been told what Antonio Marra wanted them to do, and they had also been told to keep out of sight. But now they had a body to deal with, and they had to make it disappear.

'We don't know whether the man was dead when his companions hacked him to pieces. He was certainly dead when they buried his remains in the forest. And Marra knew that one of the men had disappeared. His dream of cultivating Chinese truffles ended at that point. He told the go-between in London that he had sent the planters home to Szechuan. This is the second crime committed by Antonio Marra. He knew that a man was dead, yet he did not inform the police.'

'Planting forbidden fruit, collusion in hiding a corpse,' said one of the journalists. 'Isn't there anything else?'

'Did the other two men go back to China?' Cangio asked him. 'There is every reason to believe that they did not.'

'How do you know?'

'The businessman in London that I mentioned before,' Cangio said, not naming Li Liü Gong to avoid confusion. 'Marra told him that the three Chinese peasants had gone home. *Three* of them, not *two* of them. The fact is that those three men have never been seen alive again.'

'What does Marra say about that?'

Cangio put down the microphone to shift a bottle of mineral water that was blocking his view of the journalist who had asked the question.

Lucia Grossi grabbed the microphone like a baton in a relay race.

'This vital aspect of the case is still being explored,' she said, emphasizing the word *vital*, as if everything that had gone before had been less important. 'Our investigation is ongoing, but further charges may well be made against Antonio Marra.'

'Is he under arrest?' another journalist asked.

Lucia Grossi held the microphone as if it were a sceptre. 'Antonio Marra is currently in intensive care. He was the victim of a vicious physical attack last night, and has suffered a cardiac arrest as a result of it. I spoke with him in the early hours of this morning, and he confirms what Ranger Cangio has just told you. My colleague, Captain Geremia Esposito, is in the same hospital, recovering from a gunshot wound which he received in the course of the action last night. I want to take this opportunity to praise his bravery, and wish him a swift recovery.'

'You were injured, too,' another journalist said.

Lucia Grossi lifted the medical sling she was wearing on her left arm.

'A scratch,' she said.

'What can you tell us about the shooting last night in Valnerina, Captain?'

Cangio saw the change of expression on Lucia Grossi's face as she opened the file in front of her. Now they were going to talk about the most 'vital' question, the 'Ndrangheta, and *she* would be doing all the talking.

Cangio settled down with the rest of the audience for the next ten minutes as Lucia Grossi rolled out the facts as they were known: the company Simone Candelora had formed with Antonio Marra; the balance in Marra's bank account before and after the agreement; the other investments made by Candelora, including an adventure park and bungee jumping in Ferentillo; part-ownership of two hotels in the nearby ski resort of Terminillo; a share in a planned shopping mall outside Foligno and in a multi-screen cinema complex near Assisi.

'Naturally, Marra Truffles was the hub of the business. Cocaine was coming in from Calabria at night under the guise of building materials for expansion of the truffle factory, while cocaine was being exported through the regional airport in the form of Marra's truffle sauce. Within a short time, the clan to which Candelora belonged would have had control of the drugs market throughout Italy and northern Europe.

'It should be stressed that Simone Candelora knew nothing of the dead Chinese man, or *men*, when he went into business with Antonio Marra and started pumping cash into the failing company.'

As Lucia Grossi paused for breath, the journalists were scribbling furiously.

'This was Candelora's big mistake. He bet on the wrong horse.'

'How did you latch on to them, Captain Grossi?'

She glanced at Cangio before she spoke.

He'd had his chance, and he hadn't taken it.

Now, it was her turn.

'There was a rattling skeleton in Antonio Marra's cupboard, and Candelora didn't see it. No member of an 'Ndrangheta clan can make a mistake like that and hope to get away with it. Those bones discovered in the woods brought Marra's world crashing down around his ears. He was living a nightmare. We were moving in on him, on the one hand; his criminal partners had him bound hand and foot, on the other. It was only a matter of time before we pinned him down.'

We?

Cangio shifted in his seat.

'If I may be allowed to float a hypothesis,' Lucia Grossi continued, 'Candelora would have been eliminated by his clan if he hadn't died during the shoot-out last night. It might have been a very slow and painful death.'

A journalist stood up to ask a question.

'Regarding the events last night, Captain Grossi,' she began. 'We also know that a security guard was unfortunately killed while doing his rounds. But what about the other victims? A man connected with Simone Candelora died in London yesterday, and you still haven't said a word about Marzio Diamante or Maria Gatti . . .'

Loredana didn't go back to Todi that night.

They ate at home they way they had always done, but something was niggling her.

'What's on you mind?' he asked.

Loredana sipped from her glass of Montefalco red.

'You told me a lie,' she said.

'Which one?' he joked, but she wasn't smiling.

'You told me your phone was broken.'

'I switched it off,' he said. 'I didn't want to be traced.'

'You were in London,' she said. 'Did you have fun?'

That made him frown. 'I was on the run from the police, trying to prove that I wasn't transporting illegal Chinese immigrants across the park. Somebody was trying to kill me. Does that sound like fun?'

He didn't tell her that he had played with the idea of never coming back.

She glared at him over the rim of her wine glass. 'Why didn't you tell me you were going there?'

So that was it. He hadn't trusted her, so now she didn't trust him entirely.

He lowered his head to catch her eye. 'Hell's bells, Lori, I was desperate. I had a lead and I had to follow it. I didn't call you for your own sake. I didn't want the *carabinieri* pestering you, as well.'

'You might have gone for good,' she said, her eyes glittering.

'I'd have told you where to find me,' he said.

'Would you?'

'Lucia Grossi wanted to arrest me . . .'

'And now she wants to protect you.'

Like a cat with a mouse, he thought, though he didn't say it.

He recalled the look on the *carabiniere*'s face as she'd shown him the letter from the Ministry of Internal Affairs informing her that she would be the head of the newly formed anti-mafia crime squad in Perugia.

She would use him, of course, but using wasn't protecting.

'She's very striking,' Lori said.

Lucia Grossi had been mobbed by journalists and photographers at the end of the press conference. A young woman in a smart uniform, a heroine, too, with a bright career ahead of her – all because of the groundwork that *he* had done.

'You know where to turn,' Lucia Grossi had said to him as they posed together for a picture, 'if the danger ever presents itself again.'

That had shaken him. The 'Ndrangheta wouldn't disappear.

They'd be back, and they would want revenge. She knew it, and so did he. She would be watching him, OK, but mainly she'd be looking out for herself and her career.

'My guardian angel?' he had joked.

'That's me,' she had said.

'By the way,' Loredana said, drawing him back to the present, 'I spoke to Linda.'

'How is she?' he asked.

He hadn't seen Marzio's wife since the funeral.

'Grateful for what you said about Marzio doing his duty, and paying with his life.'

'It's the truth,' he said, though he knew it wasn't the whole truth.

If Marzio had told him what was going on at Marra Truffles, things might have turned out differently. Marzio might still be alive.

On the other hand, they might both be dead.

'. . . it's all pretty clear now,' Lori was saying. 'They murdered Maria Gatti because she knew too much from Marra, right? You know, Seb, there's one thing I still can't figure out. What was Marzio doing there alone at night?'

Would they ever know what Marzio had been doing there? Had he realised what Antonio Marra was up to, staking out the truffle reserve when he ran into the *'Ndranghetisti*?

He sipped from his glass.

The wine was good, but not great.

'He must have heard more gossip, like the first time: elves and goblins, witches and wizards. He would have gone to have a look.'

'So why didn't he tell you?'

'He knew I wouldn't fall for that rubbish,' Cangio said. 'Maybe he wanted to be certain of the facts before he told me.'

'Linda really thought that he had something going on the side. You know? A woman. That's why she was so grateful to you, Seb. You put it down to a sense of duty, courage, bad luck.'

Marzio the hero, Marzio the unfaithful?

He would have stood by Marzio, right or wrong.

'Linda told me something funny,' Lori said. 'Marzio couldn't stand you when you first came here. Did you know that? He used to call you the London laddie, thought you were really stuck up. Still, she said he learnt to love you in the end.'

She reached across the table, took hold of his hand. 'Talking of which,' she said, 'it's been three weeks. Oh, Seb, I've missed you so much.'

That was when his phone rang the first time.

'Let it ring,' she said. 'What I've got in mind won't wait.'

He did let it ring. He couldn't wait, either.

It was after ten o'clock when the phone rang again.

It was on the bedside table, purring and vibrating.

Lori was beneath him. She was purring and vibrating, too.

'Leave it!' Lori said.

The telephone rang again at midnight.

Lori was asleep by then. She turned on her side, growled incoherently.

'I have to answer it,' he said. 'It might be important.'

'Sebastiano Cangio?'

Cangio didn't recognise the voice, but there was no mistaking the harsh, lazy vowels or the nasal accent. It was from Calabria in the south.

'My friends call me Seb,' he said quietly into the phone.

'Dead men don't have friends,' the voice hissed.

There was long silence, and then the line clicked.

Lori groaned and half opened her eyes. 'Who was it?'

'No one,' Cangio said. 'Just an old friend.'

She didn't hear him. She was snoring lightly.

They'd be back.

The 'Ndrangheta wouldn't forget.

Ever . . .